JESSICA HART
Honeymoon with the Boss

ESCAPE
AROUND
the
WORLD

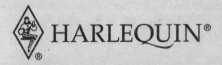

HARLEQUIN®

TORONTO • NEW YORK • LONDON
AMSTERDAM • PARIS • SYDNEY • HAMBURG
STOCKHOLM • ATHENS • TOKYO • MILAN • MADRID
PRAGUE • WARSAW • BUDAPEST • AUCKLAND

PLEASE RECYCLE
THIS PRODUCT IS RECYCLABLE

Recycling programs
for this product may
not exist in your area.

ISBN-13: 978-0-373-17590-1

HONEYMOON WITH THE BOSS

First North American Publication 2009.

Copyright © 2009 by Jessica Hart.

This edition published by arrangement with Harlequin Books S.A.

® and TM are trademarks of the publisher. Trademarks indicated with
® are registered in the United States Patent and Trademark Office, the
Canadian Trade Marks Office and in other countries.

www.eHarlequin.com

Printed in U.S.A.

Jessica Hart was born in West Africa, and has suffered from itchy feet ever since, traveling and working around the world in a wide variety of interesting but very lowly jobs. All of them have provided inspiration on which to draw when it comes to the settings and plots of her stories. Now she lives a rather more settled existence in York, U.K., where she has been able to pursue her interest in history, although she still yearns sometimes for wider horizons. If you'd like to know more about Jessica, visit her Web site at www.jessicahart.co.uk.

Look out for a Christmas treat from Jessica Hart in November with
Under the Boss's Mistletoe

This one is for Julia, who was there at the start

CHAPTER ONE

'WHERE would you like to go on honeymoon?'

Imogen paused in surprise, her arm still extended in the act of handing her boss a folder of letters across the desk. 'Honeymoon?' she repeated cautiously, wondering if she had heard correctly.

It was unlike Tom Maddison to ask personal questions, let alone one so unexpected. Sometimes on a Monday morning he remembered to ask her if she had had a good weekend, but never as if he cared about the answer and she always said 'Yes, thank you' in reply, even if it had been a disaster—as, frankly, it often was.

'Yes, honeymoon,' said Tom with an edge of impatience. He took the folder and opened it. 'You know, after you get married.'

'Er…I'm not getting married,' said Imogen.

Chance would be a fine thing, she thought wryly. All her friends seemed to be settling down, but she was obviously doomed to remain single—and it wasn't for lack of trying, whatever her best friend, Amanda, might say. Ever since Andrew had announced his engagement, she had thrown herself into the dating game, but no matter how promising her date seemed at first, Imogen always ended up making an excuse to leave early.

'Pretend that you are,' said Tom, skimming the first letter and scrawling his signature at the bottom before looking up at her with the piercingly light eyes that always reminded Imogen of stainless steel, so cool and unyielding were they.

He put down his pen. 'You're a woman,' he said, as if noticing the fact for the first time, which it probably was, Imogen thought. She was resigned now to the fact that, as far as Tom Maddison was concerned, she was little more than a walking, talking piece of office equipment.

'I have it on good authority that most women start planning their dream weddings when they're about six,' he said, 'so you must have given it some thought.'

'That's true, but at six you're only interested in pretty dresses,' Imogen pointed out. 'You're not that concerned about the groom at that stage, let alone the honeymoon.'

Tom frowned as he pulled the next letter towards him. 'So you haven't thought about it since then?'

'Well, I wouldn't say *that*,' she admitted scrupulously, 'but my fantasies have never gone beyond getting married. Sadly, I've never been in a position where there's any point in planning a honeymoon.'

'You are now.' Tom cast a cursory glance over the letter and signed it before reaching for the next one.

'Pardon?'

'I want you to plan a honeymoon,' he said, his pen moving briskly over the paper.

'But…who for?'

'For me,' said Tom, as if it were obvious.

'For *you*?'

Imogen stared at him. She shouldn't be surprised, she realised. Tom Maddison was thirty-six, single, straight and very, very rich. Why wouldn't he get married?

It wasn't as if he was unattractive, either. You couldn't call him handsome exactly, but he was tall and powerfully built and attractive in a way she couldn't quite explain. His stern face was dominated by a strong nose and those strange light eyes under formidable brows. So, no, he wasn't handsome. And yet…

And yet there was something about the line of his mouth that made the breath stick in her throat sometimes, something about the big, square, capable hands and the angle of his cheek and jaw that prickled excitingly under her skin and sent a little shiver snaking down her spine.

Offset against that was the fact that she had worked for Tom Maddison for six months without any indication that he had any emotions at all. Not once had he mentioned his personal life. It was only thanks to her friend Sue in Human Resources that Imogen even knew that he was single.

She knew all about his professional reputation, though. In the City, they called him the Iceman. He was famous for the chilly precision of his negotiations and his cold-blooded approach to the failing companies that he was brought in to turn around. She knew Tom had been in New York for a number of years, transforming the fortunes of a succession of firms familiar from the Dow-Jones Index, and that he had been lured back to London at a reputedly gigantic salary to be CEO of Collocom, which had been struggling in the competitive communications market.

But really, that was all she knew. Imogen had never met anyone so driven and focused. It was like working for a machine.

Maybe that wasn't quite fair, she amended mentally. He was too brusque and impatient to be a machine. He was tough, even ruthless, but he was absolutely straight too. Tom Maddison wasn't a man who played games, and she admired that. With Tom, what you saw was what you got.

Except now it turned out that there was another side to him. 'You're getting married?' she asked him, just in case she had misunderstood. It was hard to imagine Tom unbending enough to even smile at a woman, let alone ask her to marry him. He must have had a conversation about something other than work. Amazing.

'Didn't I tell you?'

'No,' she said with careful restraint, 'you didn't.'

She was only his temporary PA, but he might have told her, she thought. Subsiding onto the chair, Imogen studied him across the desk as he scanned another letter and wondered what his fiancée was like.

Thin, no doubt. And probably beautiful, she decided glumly.

Funny how men with millions to squander never chose to spend them on average-looking girls who could do with losing a few pounds, wasn't it?

'Well…congratulations!' she said brightly. 'When did all this happen?'

'At New Year.' Tom looked uncomfortable with the personal turn of the conversation.

'When you were in New York?' Imogen asked, surprised. He had certainly gone on his own—she knew because she had booked his ticket—and he didn't seem the type to spend a romantic weekend with a stranger, let alone rush into marriage.

'I've known Julia for nearly a year,' said Tom, as if reading her mind. He signed the last letter and sat turning the pen between his fingers with a brooding expression, giving a very bad impression of a besotted lover. 'But we didn't get together until just before I came back to London four months ago.'

'Why didn't you say anything before?'

'There didn't seem to be any need. We weren't going to get married until next year. Julia is a financial analyst, and she obviously has to sort out what's going to happen about her job if she moves over here, so I thought we had plenty of time.'

'Oh.' Imogen wasn't sure what else to say. It certainly

didn't sound like a mad, passionate love affair, but perhaps Tom was different behind closed doors.

With a mouth like that, it would be a shame if he wasn't.

'So when are you getting married?' she asked after a moment.

'In six weeks.'

'Six *weeks*!' Maybe it was a mad, passionate affair after all! 'Gosh, that's not long.'

'I know.'

Tom could hear the glumness in his own voice, and pulled himself up. He ought to be sounding more enthusiastic at the prospect. After all, getting married had been his idea.

It had made perfect sense at the time. Julia was a high-flyer, like him. She was beautiful, intelligent, successful. *Independent.* To Tom, she had seemed everything he wanted in a woman. Their relationship had been mutually satisfying, with neither making any demands on the other, and Tom couldn't imagine ever meeting anyone who would fit into his life with so little effort.

But that was before he had asked her to marry him and wedding fever had gripped her, transforming her in an instant from a cool, competent businesswoman into a neurotic fiancée, obsessed with dresses and guest lists and flowers and *fuss*. It was all very alarming, and Tom just hoped that once the wedding was over, Julia would revert to normal.

'Julia has set her heart on getting married at Stavely Castle,' he told Imogen, who was obviously wondering what the rush was. 'We just assumed it would be a year before we could book it, but it turns out that they've had a last-minute cancellation, so Julia jumped at the opportunity.'

That cancellation had thrown out all Tom's calculations. He had planned his proposal with care, just as he planned everything. He preferred his life under strict control. He didn't do spontaneous. So he had thought it all out, weighed up the advantages and disadvantages and prepared exactly what he would say to Julia. He had expected her to say yes, and she had.

What he hadn't expected was her excitement. He had assumed that they could carry on much as before for a while, with Julia's job in Manhattan and his work in London. There was no hurry. They could have a year or so to get used to being engaged and plan the perfect wedding with precision.

But Julia had thrown his plans into disarray. She had thrown herself into planning the wedding with alarming enthusiasm, her ideas becoming more and more extravagant by the day, and once she had heard that the castle would be available so soon, there was no stopping her.

Tom couldn't understand it at all. He had thought that Julia shared his pragmatic attitude to marriage. She had certainly seemed to agree that they could have a successful relationship based on mutual respect, admiration and attraction. It wasn't as if she was a silly, romantic girl expecting him to start gushing about love and all that hearts and flowers stuff. Which just made her enthusiasm for the wedding all the more baffling.

'It's all very exciting,' said Imogen encouragingly.

'Yes,' Tom agreed, but he knew that he didn't sound very excited. It was all right for Imogen. *Her* life hadn't been thrown into disorder.

'Julia is coming over next week to start planning the wedding,' he told her. 'She'll be dividing her time between here and New York, so she may need your help arranging things.'

'Of course,' said Imogen. 'Whatever I can do to help.'

'You can sort out this honeymoon business for a start,' said Tom, flicking open a file, evidently having had enough personal interaction. 'Julia's dealing with the wedding, but she tells me it's up to me to organise the honeymoon.'

'It's traditional for the groom to do that,' Imogen agreed, wondering a little at the undercurrent of irritation in his voice.

Poor Julia. She wondered if his fiancée had any idea of just how unexcited Tom was about his wedding.

'I don't know anything about honeymoons,' he was grumbling.

'It's not that hard,' said Imogen with just a hint of asperity. 'It's just a holiday. You'll want a chance to relax after the wedding, so all you need to do is find somewhere romantic where you can be alone.'

Tom frowned. 'What do you mean by romantic?'

Imogen only just stopped herself from rolling her eyes in time. 'That depends on you. Everyone's got a different idea of what's romantic. What does romance mean to you?'

'It's no use asking me,' he said unhelpfully. 'I haven't got a clue.'

Well, there was a surprise!

Imogen sighed. 'Just choose somewhere relaxing, in that case.'

'It's got to be "special".' Tom used his fingers to put hooks around the word, barely able to contain his discomfort with the idea. 'I can't just book it as if it were a normal holiday. Julia is obviously expecting me to arrange something fabulous.'

'I expect she is.'

'I haven't got time to research fabulous holidays,' Tom objected.

He studied Imogen with critical grey eyes. When he had first arrived at Collocom Imogen had been assigned as his temporary assistant until he appointed a PA of his own.

At first sight, he hadn't been impressed, Tom had to admit. She was younger and infinitely more casual than any secretary he had had before, and she had no experience of working at a senior executive level. As far as Tom could work out, she had drifted into secretarial work and was utterly lacking in ambition. It was symptomatic of the failing firm that the best assistance they could offer their new Chief Executive was a temp whose only relevant experience was a two-week assignment in Human Resources, he had thought disapprovingly.

With that wayward brown hair and relaxed approach to the dress code, Imogen always seemed faintly messy to Tom. Her desk was an absolute disgrace, for instance, and in spite of her temporary status she appeared to have an encyclopaedic knowledge of every member of staff's social life. If Tom hadn't had his hands full taking over the reins of a company whose shares were plummeting in value on a daily basis, he would have insisted on a more professional PA, but stopping the slide and turning Collocom round was his priority for now.

When he had the time, he would be looking to appoint someone qualified and experienced who would act as a professional PA but, in the meantime, Imogen had proved to be surprisingly competent. Tom might wish that she looked a little sleeker, a little crisper, but she was a more than adequate substitute in most things, so he had postponed the decision about replacing her for now. Her image might be unprofessional, but she got the job done, and for Tom that was what mattered most.

'You're a sensible woman,' he told her. 'I'm prepared to go on your recommendation.'

Sensible? It wasn't exactly a compliment to make the heart beat faster, was it? thought Imogen, disgruntled. Why couldn't he think of her as glamorous, or mysterious, or sexy, or exciting? Anything but *sensible*!

Still, it would amuse Amanda, who was always telling her how very *un*-sensible she was when it came to men.

Tom Maddison might look like the kind of man you yearned to sweep you off your feet, but a girl wanted a *little* romance. A man who thought sensible was a compliment and was clearly baffled by the idea of a romantic holiday wouldn't be that much fun to be with in reality, no matter how toe-curling his mouth, or spine-shivering his hands.

No, some men were better in your fantasies than in real life. In her fantasies, Tom had slowly unbuttoned her blouse and pressed hot kisses to her throat. He had pressed her up against a door and reduced her to a puddle of lust with the merest graze of his fingers. *My God, but you're beautiful!* he had cried as he'd thrown her across the bed.

Not *once* in her fantasies had he told her she was a sensible woman!

It would serve Tom Maddison right if she recommended a B&B in Skegness as the perfect honeymoon destination for sensible people! Not that she could do that to the unknown Julia, who obviously had a lot to put up with from her fiancé. Imogen was beginning to really feel for the poor woman.

'I *did* read about a lovely place the other day,' she told Tom.

It had been a fairly typical evening in the flat; Imogen lay on the sofa, flicking through magazines while Amanda painted her nails, both of them bemoaning their lack of a glamorous social life while secretly relieved that neither of them had to miss the latest episode of *Eastenders*. Imogen had seen the piece about the ultimate romantic getaways and shown it to Amanda, who had sighed enviously and nearly passed out when she saw how much it cost.

'It was terribly expensive, though.' Imogen felt she should warn Tom.

He waved a dismissive hand, as if nothing were too much to pay to save him from having to think about a romantic destination for himself.

It probably wasn't, thought Imogen. She didn't deal with his personal finances, but it was common knowledge that Tom Maddison was worth millions. It wasn't as if he ever spent any of them, either. All he seemed to do was work. She never booked fancy restaurants or theatre tickets or arranged for him to fly in private jets or cruise in luxury yachts.

He went to New York occasionally, but Imogen had always assumed that was for work. She had obviously been wrong about that. Perhaps Tom lavished jewels and expensive gifts on Julia? Imogen couldn't imagine it, but she might be wrong about that too.

'If money is no object, Coconut Island was described as the ultimate place for a romantic getaway,' she said. 'It's tiny, with just one incredibly stylish house and a little jetty, and you can hire the whole island just for yourself. There's a luxury hotel on a bigger island nearby, and they send someone over on a boat every day to service the house and stock the fridge with fabulous food. They'll stay and cook for you if you want, but most people there are honeymooners, and they just want to be on their own.

'I saw a picture of it in this magazine,' Imogen went on, remembering. 'It looked absolutely fabulous! There was this perfect turquoise lagoon with a white sand beach and a hammock under the coconut palms…'

Clutching the pile of papers she still held to her chest, she sighed dreamily at the memory of that picture. 'Honestly, it was paradise! I'd love to go somewhere like that, where there's nothing to do all day but laze and swim and read and…'

About to say *make love*, she trailed off awkwardly, wondering if that might be getting a bit intimate, given that her exchanges with Tom had so far been limited entirely to business matters. He wasn't the kind of boss you could chat to about sex.

'…and…er…well, you know…' she finished uncomfortably.

Tom lifted an eyebrow at Imogen's blush. 'I know,' he agreed in a dry voice and, for the first time ever, she could swear she caught a glint of amusement in the cool grey eyes. It changed his expression in a quite startling way, and Imogen felt her pulse give an odd little kick.

It was amazing what a difference a glimpse of humour made, she reflected. If she had seen *that* look before, her fantasies might have been a lot more dangerous! Just as well he was safely engaged now.

The next moment, though, he had reverted to type. 'It sounds fine,' he said briskly. 'Book it for me.'

Imogen hesitated. This was his honeymoon they were talking about. 'Wouldn't you rather do it yourself?'

'No,' said Tom with emphasis, 'I'd *rather* get on with some work.'

'But a honeymoon is such a personal thing,' she protested.

'Yes, and you're my *personal* assistant,' he pointed out. 'That means you assist me personally, so I suggest that's what you do. Now, the wedding is on…'

To Imogen's amazement, he actually consulted his computer about a date that ought to be engraved on his heart. 'Ah, yes, twenty-seventh of February. Julia is talking about having it at some castle in Gloucestershire, but we can get to Heathrow easily enough from there, so book a flight that night.

'I don't want to know about how much everything costs,' he added as Imogen opened her mouth. 'I can't be bothered with the details. Just book whatever you think and charge it to my account.'

'Very well,' said Imogen, the perfect PA once more. 'If that's what you want.'

'What I *want*,' said Tom grouchily, 'is not to be distracted. We've got an important contract to negotiate before I can get married, so let's get on with that.'

* * *

'And I've booked the honeymoon for you,' Imogen finished after handing Tom the last message. He had been out of the office in meetings all day, and the phone had been ringing constantly.

'Good, good,' said Tom absently, flicking through the messages. He was still wearing his overcoat, and his shoulders still glistened with raindrops in the harsh overhead light.

'Don't you want the details?'

He frowned. 'I suppose I'd better have them,' he decided. 'Julia might ask what I've arranged. Can you put it all in a file for me?'

'I've got it here.' Imogen handed the file over the desk. 'I do hope you'll enjoy it,' she said. 'I can't think of anywhere I'd rather be, especially with the weather the way it is at the moment,' she added, nodding to where the January rain was still splattering against the window.

Tom only grunted as he opened the file and scanned the arrangements that she had typed up. His ferocious brows rose at the cost, Imogen noticed, but to her relief he made no comment. What would it be like to barely blink at spending a hefty five-figure sum on a holiday?

He turned to the next page. 'Leaving on the twenty-seventh...' his voice sharpened '...back on the nineteenth of *March*?'

'You told me to book whatever I thought would be most appropriate,' she reminded him.

'I can't believe you thought it would be appropriate for me to be away from the office for *three weeks*!'

Imogen refused to quail. 'It's your honeymoon,' she said. 'It's a special time. It's important to get your marriage off to the right start if you *can* afford it, as you obviously can.'

'I'm not talking about money,' he said impatiently. 'It's time I can't afford.'

'I'm not talking about money either,' said Imogen.

'Collocom isn't going to fall apart if you're not here for three weeks, so you can afford the time. It's a question of priorities. What matters more, Collocom or your marriage?'

Tom eyed his PA with something close to dislike. He knew how he was supposed to reply to *that*!

He thought wistfully of the days when he and Julia had had a successful long-distance relationship. Their weekends in New York had been mutually satisfying. Julia had her own busy life, and respected his space. He hadn't been expected then to think about all this emotional stuff, or to reassess his priorities.

He hadn't counted on all these changes. If he'd known, would he ever have thought about marriage? Tom wondered with an inward sigh.

It would be fine, he reassured himself. Julia was an incredible woman, and he was lucky to have met her. She would understand about the honeymoon.

'I'll talk to Julia about it,' he told Imogen, closing the file with a snap. 'Then you can rearrange the flights.'

But Julia was thrilled when he told her about Coconut Island. 'Thank you for choosing somewhere so romantic, honey,' she enthused. 'And three weeks alone! I can't wait! Won't it be wonderful to spend that time together and get to know each other properly?'

Tom thought they *did* know each other. Why else would they be getting married?

He had been hoping that Julia would want to cut the honeymoon short. A drive for success was something they had in common—or, at least, it had been until Julia had gone wedding crazy. Now it appeared she would rather loll around on a beach for three weeks than get back to work! Wouldn't she want to know what was happening in her absence? Wouldn't she be concerned about deals being made without her, or the challenges and opportunities she would miss while she was sitting under some coconut palm?

This was Imogen's fault, Tom thought darkly. If she hadn't booked such a long stay, Julia would have been perfectly happy to return to normal after a week.

When Imogen asked him if he wanted her to rearrange the flights, he snapped at her but had to concede that the dates should stay as she had booked.

'Leave it as it is,' he snarled.

'Oh-kay…good,' said Imogen, eyeing him warily. Being engaged didn't seem to be suiting him at all.

Tom's foul mood continued for the next couple of days. He was so grouchy that Imogen began to wonder if Julia had called the engagement off. If Tom was like this with her, Imogen wouldn't have blamed her!

Not that she had any intention of asking him if everything was all right. She valued her head too much. The only thing to do when Tom was like this was to keep her head down and be glad that she was only a very temporary secretary.

Think of the money, Imogen told herself. She was earning good money here and her travel fund was looking positively healthy. As soon as Tom got round to appointing a new PA she would be off to Australia and someone else could deal with him. Good luck to her!

It appeared, though, that the engagement was very much still on. Imogen was squinting at her shorthand a couple of days later when the phone rang.

'Chief Executive's office.'

'Hi, is that Imogen?' The warm American voice spilled out of the phone. 'This is Julia, Tom's fiancée, here. Tom said you might be able to help me with a few little things.'

Those 'few little things' turned out to be a list of details to check that extended to three pages. Imogen rolled her eyes as she scribbled down notes, but she had to admit that Julia was very friendly and appreciative. Unlike Tom, she was obviously thrilled at the prospect of a wedding.

'I'm having a dress made here,' she told Imogen excitedly. 'It is so-o-o-o beautiful! I knew exactly what I wanted. In fact, I'll email you the design—you're being so helpful, I'm thinking of you as a kind of cyber bridesmaid! Would you like to see it?'

Imogen had little choice but to murmur politely that she would love to.

'Don't show Tom, though! It's unlucky for him to see it before the wedding.'

Imogen tried, and failed, to imagine poring girlishly over a dress design with her boss. Tom must be very different with Julia if she thought he'd have the slightest interest in what anyone wore.

'I won't.'

'Now, I've booked Stavely Castle for the wedding and reception,' said Julia. 'I visited last time I was in England and it was just so romantic. I decided there and then if I ever got married, that's where I wanted the wedding!'

She rattled on, wanting Imogen to book a string quartet, find a supply of fresh rose petals, put her in touch with a cake designer, draw up a list of hotels in the area…

'You're so sweet to help me out like this,' she told Imogen. 'It's difficult to sort out details like this from New York, and I'm just so busy at the moment, what with sorting out everything here before I come over to London. I had no idea how much work organising a wedding would be on top of it all!'

'It's a lot to do at such short notice,' Imogen agreed, reflecting that Julia wasn't the only busy one. Sadly, they didn't all have fiancés with assistants they could fob off with all the time-consuming jobs!

'I know, it's crazy, isn't it?' Julia's laugh sounded a little

wild to Imogen. 'But Stavely Castle suddenly had a cancellation and it just seemed *meant* somehow. As I said to Tom,
when you know you've found the right person, why wait?'

Imogen murmured something noncommittal. It seemed to
her that if you wanted a spontaneous wedding, it made sense
to keep things simple and let the rose petals and the string
quartets go. Still, it wasn't her wedding, and Julia and Tom had
plenty of money to throw at the problem, which always helped.

'How *is* Tom?' Julia was asking.

'Er, he's fine,' said Imogen, wondering if she was expected
to report that her boss was working himself into a frenzy of
excitement about the wedding. 'Working hard. You know
what he's like.'

Julia laughed. 'I know. Isn't he a darling? He's so British
sometimes!'

'Absolutely,' Imogen agreed, boggling at the phone. Tom
Maddison, a *darling*? Julia must be in love!

'Is he there?'

'Of course. I'll put you through.'

Putting Julia on hold, Imogen buzzed Tom. 'I've got Julia
on the line.'

'Julia?' he snapped.

'Your fiancée,' she reminded him.

'What does she want?'

'She didn't say. I imagine she wants to talk to you.'

'I can't talk now,' he said irritably. 'Can't it wait? Tell her
I'm in a meeting.'

'I've already said that I would put her through.'

He made an exasperated sound. 'Oh, very well.'

Imogen grimaced as she put down the phone. Some darling!

She felt sorry for Julia. There had been a feverishness to
the other woman's voice that boded ill for a measured conversation with her fiancé. A few minutes' conversation had

been enough to show Imogen that Julia was a control freak, and already stressed by having to organise the perfect wedding at long distance. Right now, Julia needed calm reassurance, but Imogen was afraid she was unlikely to get it from Tom in his current mood.

Five minutes later, Tom banged out of his office, his mood clearly even worse than she had feared.

'This wedding business is getting out of control,' he snarled. 'I haven't got time to talk about invitations and vows and rehearsal dinners! And *you're* spending far too much time on it, too,' he added accusingly.

'I don't mind,' she said quickly. 'It'll be easier when Julia is here.'

'I hope to God you're right!'

'You have to make allowances.' Imogen was beginning to feel like a counsellor. She certainly seemed to spend more time talking to Tom and to Julia than they were talking to each other. 'A wedding is a big deal for any woman,' she tried to placate Tom. 'Julia's giving up her life in New York to be with you, so it's going to be an even more emotional time than usual for her. I know it seems like a lot of stress at the moment, but it will be worth it when you're married, won't it?'

Tom stopped pacing and imagined a time when he and Julia were safely married. Everything would be calm again, and he would go home every night to a beautiful, accomplished wife who understood what made a successful relationship and who would support him professionally and personally. He could rely on Julia to always say the right thing, and do the right thing. She was neat and orderly and sensible—except when it came to weddings, it seemed.

Perhaps Imogen was right, and it was just the stress of arranging a wedding at short notice that was making Julia so uncharacteristically emotional. Once this damned wedding was over, surely she would go back to the way she had been before?

It had taken Tom a long time to find just the right wife. Julia wouldn't normally expect him to be all lovey-dovey. They had come to a very clear agreement about what they both wanted from marriage, so if it didn't work with her, it was never going to work with anyone.

No, Julia was perfect. He didn't want to lose her now.

He would just have to be more patient, Tom decided. He would try harder to show an interest in the wedding if that was what Julia wanted.

He could feel Imogen's stern eye on him and remembered her question. *It will be worth it, won't it?*

'Of course it will,' he said.

CHAPTER TWO

IMOGEN waved at the girls on Reception and pressed the button to call the lift. This was Tom's last day in the office before the wedding, and the staff had planned a surprise champagne reception later that afternoon to wish him well.

She hoped Tom would appreciate the gesture and manage a smile for them. Most of the staff were terrified of his brusque manner, but they respected him, too. He was tough, but fair, and no one was in any doubt that he had transformed Collocom in the six months he had been there. Their boss's wedding was an excuse to celebrate a much more secure future for them all.

It had been a busy few weeks. Imogen had spent most of them chasing up string quartets and florists and photographers. She was an expert now on everything from the design of the place settings to special licence arrangements, and she was on first-name terms with the staff at Stavely Castle after ringing on a daily basis to change or check endless details. Perhaps when she got back from her travels she could set up as a wedding planner?

There had been no word from Julia for a couple of days now, which was odd. Tom's fiancée had been backwards and forwards between New York and London for the past few weeks, but ten days ago she had arrived, she said, to stay. Imogen had arranged for her to lease a fabulous flat in Chelsea Harbour so that she could prepare for the wedding, but she had still been on the phone several times a day. Imogen just hoped that—finally!—everything was ready and Julia could stop fretting.

Tom's fiancée was very lovely, as slender as predicted, and beautifully dressed. There was a glossiness and a sheen to her that made Imogen feel gauche and faintly shabby in comparison. They were probably much the same age, but Julia was so much more sophisticated she seemed to come from a different world, one where first-class travel and designer clothes were the norm, and a million miles from Imogen's life sharing a chaotic flat in south London.

In spite of the differences between them, Julia was determined to treat Imogen as her new best friend when they'd finally met in the office one day. She was warm and friendly, embarrassingly so at times, but Imogen sensed a tension to her and a frenetic undercurrent to her obsession with wedding arrangements, as if she were wound up like a tightly coiled spring. Imogen hoped she would be able to relax enough to enjoy the wedding.

Julia had brought Imogen a beautiful scarf to thank her for all her work. 'I do hope you'll come to the wedding, Imogen,' she said, kissing her on both cheeks when she first met her. 'It would mean the world to Tom and me if you were there. Wouldn't it, Tom?'

It had clearly never crossed Tom's mind to care one way or another, but he nodded. 'Of course,' he agreed. 'I know how hard Imogen has worked to make sure it all happens.'

There was a very faint edge to his voice. Imogen knew just how often he had been exasperated to find her tied up with wedding arrangements when he needed her to do something else, but she had to admit that he'd been making much more of an effort lately. She wondered if Julia realised quite how hard he was trying.

Julia had confided to Imogen in one of her many phone calls that she had wondered at one time if Tom had been having second thoughts about getting married. 'But he's been so sweet lately that I can see I was silly to have worried,' she said. 'He rings twice a day, and sends me a red rose every morning just so I know he's thinking about me.'

Julia sighed with satisfaction. As well she might, Imogen reflected. She had arranged the delivery of the single roses herself and knew exactly how much it cost. Her mind boggled at the idea of Tom being sweet. He must really love Julia if he was prepared to change to such an extent, she thought wistfully.

She tried hard to be happy for them. It wasn't Julia's fault if she was thin, beautiful, wealthy, glamorous and had a man like Tom Maddison at her feet.

It wasn't her fault if Imogen couldn't stick to a diet, devoured a whole packet of chocolate digestives at a sitting and was reduced to dates with men who explained exactly how a mobile phone worked or who actually thought she would be interested in a detailed account of the intergalactic battles in *Star Wars*.

'Your trouble is that you're too picky,' Amanda was always telling her. 'You're looking for a prince, and he's just not going to turn up. You've got to be prepared to compromise a bit.'

'I don't want to compromise.' Imogen could be stubborn too. 'I want what I had with Andrew.'

Amanda sighed. 'You've got to get over him, Imo.'

'I *am* over him.' She thought she was, anyway. 'I know he's happy with Sara. I know he's not going to come back. But when you've had the perfect relationship, it's hard to settle for anything less.'

'If it had been the perfect relationship, Andrew wouldn't have broken it off,' Amanda invariably pointed out.

It was a good point. Imogen knew her friend was right, and she really *was* trying to meet someone new. It was just that the men she met seemed lacking in even the hint of a spark.

Still, perhaps she should give them more of a chance, Imogen had decided only the week before. Look at how Tom had changed and was trying hard to please Julia. He must be in love with her if he was prepared to make that kind of effort.

Sick of yearning after the unattainable, as Amanda put it, Imogen had vowed to try harder. There was no reason why she shouldn't find someone she could have a real relationship with, perhaps even someone who might like to come travelling with her, but it hadn't been going well. Last night she had let Amanda's boyfriend set her up on yet another blind date, this time with an engineer who had spent most of his time telling her about his multiple allergies.

No wonder she was feeling depressed this morning.

It was nothing to do with the fact that Tom Maddison was getting married in a couple of days.

The lights were on in both offices when she went in. That meant Tom was here already. He had probably been here since at least seven, in fact, the way he usually was. He wasn't the kind of man who would take it easy just because he was getting married.

Imogen tested a smile in the mirror as she hung up her coat. It didn't look very convincing. She tried again, adding a little sparkle to her eyes. Better. She could almost pass for a girl who was genuinely pleased for her boss.

She *wanted* to be. Tom might be grouchy at times, but she admired his self-discipline and integrity. He wasn't the friendliest of bosses, but you always knew where you were with him.

And he never mentioned an allergy or gave the slightest indication he had even seen *Star Wars*. He deserved a beautiful wife like Julia.

'Good morning,' she said brightly, as she knocked and went into his office. 'Your last day before the wedding! Where would you like me to start?'

Tom looked up from the papers on his desk, and Imogen's heart plummeted as she saw that his face looked as if it were carved out of stone.

'You can start by cancelling the wedding,' he said.

There was a catastrophic silence.

'*Cancel* it?' said Imogen, aghast, hoping against hope that she had misheard.

Tom nodded curtly. 'Pull the plug on everything.'

'But…what on earth has happened? Where's Julia?'

'On her way back to New York.' He looked at his watch. 'Probably taking off right now.'

'She'll come back,' said Imogen, thinking that Julia would have to turn round as soon as she landed to get back in time for the wedding. 'It must just be last-minute nerves.'

'She doesn't want to get married,' said Tom flatly. 'No, that's not quite right,' he corrected himself. 'She *does* want to get married, just not to me.'

No matter how hard he tried, he couldn't keep the bitterness from his voice.

Imogen had been standing as if rooted to the spot, but at that she turned to close the door and, without waiting to be invited, sat down across the desk.

'Are you sure there hasn't been some kind of mistake?' she asked carefully. 'Is it possible you've misunderstood what the problem is?'

Tom gave a harsh, mirthless laugh. 'Oh, no, she was crystal clear. I misunderstood the whole situation, it turns out, but not what she wants to do now.'

He couldn't bear to be pitied. Swinging his chair round so that he wouldn't have to look at the sympathy in Imogen's face, he stared out of the window at the bleak February morning. It suited his mood exactly.

'All of Julia's family and friends are over for the wedding, and she'd arranged to spend the evening with them, so I wasn't expecting to see her. But she turned up at my door at ten o'clock and said that we had to talk,' he told Imogen. 'It wasn't the easiest of scenes. She said that she was sorry, but she couldn't marry me because she was going to marry Patrick.'

'Patrick?' Imogen felt completely lost. This was all so unexpected it was difficult to grasp what he was telling her. 'Who's Patrick?'

'Patrick is Julia's best friend, always has been, ever since they were at college together. I met him in New York, and knew they spent lots of time together, but Julia always said that they had decided long ago not to spoil their friendship by sleeping together. It was always a platonic relationship, and they both dated other people, like me. That was one of the reasons she was always so happy with a long-distance relationship,' Tom remembered. 'When I wasn't there, she had plenty of time to spend with Patrick, just "goofing around", as she called it.'

Imogen could practically hear the quotation marks around the phrase, and she could understand his baffled distaste. Tom probably didn't even know what goofing around was.

'It turns out that Julia was in love with Patrick all along,' he went on. 'She didn't say anything because she didn't want to lose him as a friend, but she wasn't getting any younger and she decided that if she wanted to get married and have a family, as she does, she would have to make a decision to commit to someone else. That's when Muggins here came along.'

Tom couldn't look at Imogen. He was burning with humiliation, furious with himself for not realising the truth, furious with Julia for making a fool of him. She had made such a fuss about the wedding, and invited half the world, so everyone would know that he was the man too stupid to realise his fiancée was in love with someone else, too weak to convince her to stay, too inept to build a successful relationship.

Now they would all know he was a failure.

They would know he hadn't been able to control his own life.

His jaw was clenched, but he couldn't stop the betraying muscle jumping frantically in his cheek. He wanted to bellow with rage, to punch his fist into a wall, but he couldn't do that. Imogen would think he was upset and feel even sorrier for him.

'When I asked her to marry me, she thought it was a good chance to get away from New York and Patrick, and start afresh,' he went on after a moment. 'She liked me, she said, and she liked sleeping with me. She thought we had a lot in common and would make a good team. I did, too,' he remembered with bitterness. 'Once she'd made that decision, she threw herself into the whole idea of getting married.'

'To compensate for the fact that she really wanted to be marrying someone else?' Imogen said numbly. The feverish edge to Julia's planning was beginning to make more sense now. She must have been desperate to get married while she could still convince herself that she was making the right decision. No wonder she had been keen to have the wedding in England and so soon.

'She certainly fooled me.' Tom's mouth twisted as he swung round to face Imogen once more. He would show her that he was in control. 'I had no idea I wasn't the one she really wanted to marry.'

'So what changed?'

'Apparently the prospect of losing her was too much for Patrick and he came to his senses. He realised that he was in love with her, too, and probably always had been. It's quite a touching story, when you think about it.'

Tom smiled without humour. 'Patrick came over for the wedding, but when he saw Julia he told her how he felt, and then of course she realised she couldn't go through with marrying me. She said she was sorry,' he added expressionlessly.

The look in his eyes made Imogen want to cry. 'I don't know what to say. I'm so sorry,' she said helplessly.

'It's probably all for the best,' said Tom briskly. 'Better for Julia to realise that she was making a mistake now than after the wedding. At least it's saved us the hassle—and cost!—of a divorce.'

That would have been an admission of failure too. Either way, Julia would have made him look a loser.

And Tom was a winner. He didn't like losing. He never had.

He picked up his pen, almost as if he intended to get on with some work, but put it down again after a moment. The truth was, he didn't know how to deal with this. He was too angry and humiliated to work, but what else could he do?

Imogen swallowed. Tom wasn't the kind of man who went in for emotional displays but she knew how hard he must be hurting. He had tried so hard to be what Julia wanted.

'What can I do?' she asked.

'I'd be grateful if you would deal with telling everyone who needs to know.' The curtness in Tom's voice didn't quite disguise his gratitude that she was going to stick to practicalities.

'Of course.'

'Here's the key to Julia's apartment. She left it with me last night.'

He pushed a key across the desk. Imogen recognised it from when she had arranged the short-term lease of the flat. Julia had wanted somewhere to stay where she could keep her wedding dress secret from Tom.

At the time, Imogen had rolled her eyes at the extravagance, which seemed to be taking tradition to extremes, but now she marvelled that she hadn't seen the separate apartment as a warning sign. If Julia had been really in love with Tom, she wouldn't have been able to wait to move in with him. It wasn't as if he didn't have the space. Imogen had been to his penthouse flat in the Docklands to collect some papers once, and there had been more than enough room to hide a dozen wedding dresses if necessary.

'The flat is full of presents that will need to be returned. Presumably you've got a list of guests?'

Imogen nodded. 'I'll make sure they all know the wedding has been cancelled.'

'You'd better deal with Stavely Castle first.'

'I'll do that.' She got to her feet and hesitated, looking at him with concern. With anyone else, she would have offered the comfort of a hug, but she didn't think Tom would welcome a gesture like that. He wasn't a tactile man.

Still, this would be a devastating blow for a man of his pride. Imogen wished she could do something to help him, but she sensed the best thing she could do was deal with the practicalities and make as little fuss as possible.

She couldn't go without saying something, though. 'Will you be all right?' she asked after a moment.

'Of course,' he said, as brusque as ever. 'I've got plenty to do.'

'You're not really going to work, are you?'

'What else is there to do?' he said and even he could hear the bleakness in his voice.

Imogen came back a little while later with coffee and a couple of biscuits.

'I never eat biscuits,' said Tom, glancing up from his computer screen as she set them solicitously at his elbow.

'You should have something to eat.'

'I'm not an invalid, Imogen!'

'You've had a shock,' she said. 'You need the sugar.'

'I don't *need* anything!' The suggestion of neediness always caught Tom on the raw and he glared at Imogen. 'I'm perfectly all right,' he snapped. 'There's no need to treat me as if I'm about to faint or burst into tears.'

'Eat them anyway,' said Imogen, who thought it might be better if he did.

Tom Maddison was a difficult man to help. What was the point of pretending that you didn't have feelings? He had retreated behind an even more ferocious mask than usual, bottling it all up inside, and was clearly going to lash out at anyone who dared to suggest that he might be hurt, or angry, or in need of comfort.

Well, she would just have to be lashed, Imogen decided. She had been spared Tom's public humiliation, but she knew what it was like to realise that the person you loved didn't love you back and never had. It hurt. It hurt a lot and, although no one could endure it for you, it helped to have someone by your side to see you through it.

Tom would never admit that he needed anyone, but he did.

Imogen wished she knew more about his private life. If only there was a friend she could call, *someone* who would come and be there for Tom, the way Amanda had been there for her. But it looked as if it was just her.

She transferred her notebook from under her arm and flicked it open. For now, she would stick with the practicalities.

'I've spoken to the Castle, and cancelled all the arrangements there. I'm afraid that, at this stage, there's no question of any refunds,' she added apologetically.

'God, what a waste of money!' Tom threw himself back in his chair and rubbed the back of his neck as he thought of the cost. He hadn't begrudged paying for Julia's increasingly extravagant ideas, but what had been the point of it all? He had let Julia have whatever she wanted.

He hadn't realised the only thing she really wanted was Patrick.

'Then there's the honeymoon…'

Imogen hesitated about raising the matter of the honeymoon, but that had been booked and paid for too, and Tom would have to make some decision. The cost of Coconut Island was phenomenal. It would make a dent in even Tom's bank account, surely.

'I've been thinking about that,' said Tom, taking a biscuit without quite realising what he was doing. 'You said it was somewhere you'd love to go,' he reminded her.

Imogen squirmed. 'I'm sorry it turned out to be so expensive.'

But really, how was she to know Julia would turn her back on the wedding of her dreams, the holiday of a lifetime and a man like Tom? Julia must really love Patrick to give up all that, she reflected. 'I'll see if it's possible to get some money back, at least.'

If it had been her own holiday, she would have taken out insurance, but it had never occurred to her to think it would be an issue for Tom.

'I'll get on to the agents and see what the cancellation terms are,' she said.

'Don't do that,' said Tom, brushing biscuit crumbs from his fingers and making up his mind. 'I don't want you to cancel the trip.'

Imogen looked at him in concern. Surely he wasn't planning to go anyway? It would be a disaster. Every time he turned round he would be reminded that Julia wasn't there.

'I'm not sure it's a great idea for you to go on your own,' she said cautiously.

'I'm not planning to go on my own,' he said. 'You're coming with me.'

'*What?*'

'I've wasted enough money on the wedding. I've spent a bloody fortune on that island, and I'm not going to waste that too. You said you'd like to go there. Well, now's your chance.'

'But…it's booked as a honeymoon,' stammered Imogen. 'Everyone would assume that we were married.'

'Who's going to know, or care?' Tom countered. 'They're only interested in my money. It's not as if they're going to ask to see the marriage certificate when we check in.'

'Well, no, but…' Imogen looked at him despairingly. Couldn't he *see* how awkward it would be? 'I booked it as a honeymoon, so they might make a fuss when we arrive.'

'Let them,' said Tom. 'Surely the whole point of the exercise was that we would have complete privacy? This isn't some B&B where we'd have no choice but to share a bed. At least, it had better not be for the price I'm paying for it!' he added caustically. 'OK, we may have to bluff it on arrival, but after that we should have a whole island to ourselves and no one will know that we're not spending our whole time having sex.'

Imogen was mortified to feel her cheeks burning. Honestly, anyone would think she had never heard the word *sex* before! But somehow Tom talking about it made it all too easy to imagine Tom *doing* it.

She forced the image aside, not without some difficulty.

'You make it all sound so reasonable,' she protested.

'Because it is reasonable. It's a practical solution to the problem, and would be a good thing for both of us. What's not reasonable about that?'

Imogen fiddled with her pen and tried to imagine what it would be like to go on holiday with her boss. 'It would still be a bit…intimate,' she said at last.

'I don't see why—' Tom stopped as it occurred to him, somewhat belatedly, that Imogen might have a personal life of her own. He knew that she wasn't married, but there might be a man on the scene, and that might complicate matters.

He frowned. 'Are you worried about what a boyfriend might think?'

'It's not that,' said Imogen. 'There isn't anyone else at the moment.'

'Even better then,' said Tom, relieved. 'That means no one has any excuse to feel jealous or upset.'

'Maybe not, but there'll be plenty of people who'll speculate about why we're going on holiday together.'

Tom scowled. 'Who on earth is going to care?'

'The entire staff of Collocom for a start, I should think.'

'What business is it of theirs what we do?'

'None, of course, but that's not going to stop them wondering. *I'd* wonder what was going on if my boss and his secretary disappeared to a tropical island for three weeks!'

'Tell them it's a business trip,' Tom said indifferently.

'Oh, yes, like they'll believe that!'

'Frankly, I'm not concerned with what they do and don't believe,' he said with a dismissive gesture. 'The fact is that it *will* be a business trip. We'll have a whole island between us. We can take our laptops, and if we've got access to the Internet there's no reason why we shouldn't get on with some work.'

Imogen looked dubious. 'Do you think there'll be an Internet connection?' she asked, even as she realised that she had been lured into discussing details before they had really dealt with the issue at hand.

'At that price there certainly ought to be!'

'I don't know,' she said, still doubtful. 'I can't imagine many people hire a private island to work. It's meant as a romantic hideaway,' she reminded him. 'I don't think the idea is that you spend your time checking email.'

'Then you'd better find out,' said Tom, 'because I have no

intention of cutting myself off from work for three weeks. It'll be a good chance to catch up on a few projects without the distraction of endless meetings.'

Pushing back his chair, he got to his feet and prowled over to the window, where he stood looking out at the sleety rain that splattered against the glass. 'We might as well get something out of this whole fiasco.'

Imogen bit her lip as she regarded his back. Silhouetted against the window, he looked massive and solitary. Internet access, or lack of it, wasn't the problem here.

'Are you sure you've thought this through?' she asked carefully.

Tom kept his gaze on the rain. 'What do you mean?'

'Have you considered how painful it's going to be for you if I'm there instead of Julia?'

'Not as painful as forking out however many thousand pounds and having absolutely nothing to show for it,' he said, but he knew that Imogen had a point.

'I suspect it's going to be awkward to be around for a while,' he went on, not without some difficulty. 'It'll be easier for everyone if I'm not here and then they don't have to tell me they're sorry or remember not to mention anything to do with weddings.'

He hesitated, his eyes on the wet pavements far below. The sun would be shining in the Maldives, he thought. What would it be like there? He hadn't really thought about going with Julia but now he let himself imagine being there with Imogen.

It would be easier if he could work, and she could help him to do that. The beauty of modern technology was that you could work anywhere, so why not the Maldives? Imogen could be his PA there as well as here.

And while Tom might try and tell himself that he didn't care what people thought, deep down his humiliation was still raw. It would be bad enough dealing with the sympathy here without having to explain himself all over again when he turned up for a honeymoon on his own.

He could feel Imogen watching him warily.

'I could go to the island on my own,' he said, turning back to face her, his hands in his pockets, 'but then it really would be obvious that something was wrong. There would be fewer explanations if you came too.'

Dammit, he didn't want to beg! 'You've been doing all the work for this wedding, anyway,' he ploughed on. 'You deserve a break.'

'I thought I was going to work?'

'I'll be working,' he said. 'You can do what you like.'

Imogen regarded him a little helplessly. It seemed all wrong to be taking another woman's place on a honeymoon, but she sensed that Tom was too proud to ask her outright. The holiday would probably be a good thing for him, but he would lose face going alone, and she knew that would be difficult for him.

Was it so much to ask? She hated the thought of Tom being on his own at a time like this, and this way she could at least keep him company and offer support if he needed it.

And, when it came down to it, it was February and he was offering her three free weeks in luxurious surroundings in the Maldives. If nothing else, it would get her away from *Star Wars* fanatics and allergy sufferers.

She drew a breath. 'All right,' she said, 'if you really would like me to go, I'll go.'

'Fine' was all he said, but he couldn't quite conceal the flash of relief in his eyes as he sat back down at his desk, and that made her feel better, or at least as if she was doing the right thing.

'Transfer Julia's ticket into your name,' he said, 'and tell anyone who asks that we're going on a business trip.'

CHAPTER THREE

'WELCOME, Mr and Mrs Maddison, and congratulations!' The resort manager himself met Tom and Imogen as they stepped onto the jetty. The light was dazzling and the heat was both a relief and a shock after the air-conditioning on the flight. A flying boat had brought them from the airport on Malé to their base, and their luggage was already being transferred to a sleek speedboat that was waiting to take them on the last leg to Coconut Island itself.

Imogen averted her eyes from her battered old trolley bag. It was perfectly adequate for package holidays to Greece and Spain, but it looked very out of place here amongst the other designer cases and honeymooners' matching luggage sets that were being unloaded from the seaplane.

She must look as out of place as her luggage, she realised. She was very conscious of her crumpled trousers and creased top. February wasn't the best time to buy hot-weather clothes in London, so she had little choice but to bring the clothes she had worn to Greece the year before. They were cheap and cheerful, and had been perfect there, but she could see the other travellers eyeing her askance.

There was nothing cheap about this resort, where all the guests seemed to be beautifully dressed. Everyone seemed to be in couples, and they were uniformly lithe and golden and glowing with happiness.

Imogen shifted uncomfortably. In comparison, she knew she must look pasty, fat and frazzled by the tension of the last few days. There was no way anyone would take her for a radiant bride, that was for sure. They must all be wondering what on earth she was doing with someone like Tom Maddison.

Not that Tom fitted in any better than she did. He was actually wearing a suit! At least he had taken his jacket off now, but his shirtsleeves were still buttoned, his tie still knotted. Imogen wondered if he had ever been on holiday before.

Tom wasn't giving a very good impression of a newlywed either, it had to be said. His expression was as forbidding as ever, but the power of his presence was such that the resort manager had picked him unerringly from all the couples who disembarked from the seaplane as the recently married Tom Maddison, who had hired the most luxurious and expensive accommodation available.

'If you wouldn't mind completing a few formalities…' he said, politely concealing his disbelief at Tom Maddison's new wife, who was clearly not what they had been expecting.

He led them ahead of everyone else to the spectacular reception area, which was all dark wood, lush tropical plants and understated glamour. It practically reeked of money, thought Imogen, trying not to stare. Fabulously expensive hotels would be ten a penny to the new Mrs Maddison.

'As soon as this is done, you'll be taken straight to Coconut Island, where you'll be assured complete privacy during your stay,' the manager went on. He gestured towards a slim young man dressed in pristine white, who was waiting to one side. 'Ali will visit once a day and will make sure you have everything you need.'

Tom merely nodded, but Imogen felt as if she ought to

show a little more enthusiasm. 'Thank you,' she said, plastering on a big smile. 'I'm sure it will all be lovely.'

The manager, having obviously decided he wouldn't get much small talk out of Tom, turned to Imogen with a courteous smile.

'I hope you had a happy day for your wedding?'

There was a tiny pause. They had agreed on the plane that it would be easier not to go into complicated explanations, but surely it must be obvious that they weren't actually married. Imogen felt as if there must be a neon sign flashing 'liar' with an arrow pointing down right above her head, but she kept her smile in place somehow.

'Er…yes…thank you,' she said awkwardly, tucking her left hand away so that the manager wouldn't notice the glaring absence of a wedding ring.

Tom glanced up from the form he was signing and, rather to Imogen's surprise, seemed to pick up on her discomfort. Or perhaps he just didn't think she was putting on a very convincing performance, because he reached out and put his arm around her waist, pulling her into his side.

'Imogen's very tired,' he explained her lack of enthusiasm. 'She's had a busy time organising the wedding, and it was a long flight.'

'Of course, of course.' The manager beamed at them both. 'But now you are here, you can be alone together and relax.'

Oh, yes, *sure*, thought Imogen, who had rarely felt less relaxed than she did at that moment. Tom had shaken her hand when they'd first met, but she didn't think he had ever touched her since, and now his arm was warm and strong around her, holding her against a body that was leaner and harder and more solid than she could ever have imagined. His big hand rested casually, proprietorially, at her waist, exactly as a besotted husband's would, and he seemed astonishingly natural, as if he knew her body as well as his own.

Imogen's heart was pounding and her skin where she was pressed into his side, and beneath his hand, was tingling and twitching with awareness of him, of his warmth and his strength and the clean masculine smell of him. Her knees felt ridiculously weak and she was conscious of a bizarre and disturbing desire to turn into the hard security of his body, to hold him tight and burrow into him.

Her mouth dried at the very thought of it. Relax? Ha!

She managed a weak smile. 'I can't wait.'

'You must let us know if there is anything—anything at all!—we can do to make your stay more comfortable.'

Imogen wondered wildly if she could ask if he would swap Tom for a less unsettling companion, one she could chat away to without her heart thudding and thumping with the memory of what it felt like to be held against him.

She was overreacting, Imogen scolded herself. She could blame it on jet lag. This was *Tom*, for heaven's sake! Her boss.

The boss who had just had his heart broken, remember? Imogen felt a little ashamed to realise that she hadn't given Julia a thought since she'd arrived. It had been such a thrill to fly over the islands. Pressing her nose against the seaplane's window, she had gasped at the heart-stopping beauty of the scene.

They'd flown across islands fringed with dazzling white sand, while the water between them was so intensely coloured it seemed almost unreal: the deep, dark blue of the ocean beyond the reefs; bright aquamarine striped with violet and lilac over the sand bars; the pale, translucent emerald of the shallow lagoons. Far below, the little boats zipping over the sea had been tiny streaks flecking the surface with their wake, while the waves broke silently against the reef in a froth of white.

Caught up in amazement at it all, it wasn't surprising that she had forgotten Julia, but Tom wouldn't have done. How could he?

This must all be so difficult for him, she thought as, to her intense relief, Tom released her to complete the paperwork. How hard would it be to arrive in this beautiful place to spend what should have been three glorious weeks with his bride, knowing that whenever he turned his head, instead of the svelte, gorgeous Julia, he would just see his very ordinary PA? It would be like salt rubbing into the wound every time.

Imogen bit her lip. And here she was getting in a state about a brief hug! It was far, far worse for Tom. He must surely be regretting now that he had asked her to come.

She stood feeling miserably self-conscious as the resort manager outlined the arrangements that had been made for them. It was clear that Tom wasn't listening any more than she was. 'Yes, yes,' he said with a trace of impatience as he signed the last form. 'Whatever's been arranged will be fine.'

'Excellent. In that case, I'm sure you're anxious to be left alone.' The manager waved Ali over and they all trooped back down to the jetty, where the speedboat was already throbbing gently, ready for the off.

Tom put his hand lightly against her back to guide her to the steps leading down to the boat, and Imogen's heart lurched into her throat once more. Telling herself not to be so stupid, she climbed into the boat, barely noticing the hand Ali put out to steady her, but burningly aware of Tom's touch long after he had dropped his hand.

Willing the blush she could feel creeping up her cheeks to fade, Imogen sat stiffly on the luxurious seat as Tom jumped easily down into the boat and took his place beside her. She couldn't let herself get into a state whenever he touched her! The next three weeks were going to be difficult enough as it was.

Three weeks alone with him.

What on earth was she doing here? It had made a warped kind of sense that day in London when she had agreed to come. Tom had needed to get away. She would help him save face. It was a purely business arrangement.

True, Amanda hadn't seemed convinced. 'Business?' she said when Imogen told her that she would be away for three weeks. 'On a tropical island?'

'It'll be just like being in the office,' Imogen said. 'But with better weather.'

'Sure.' Amanda's tone reeked scepticism.

'It will,' she insisted. 'I've got to take my laptop. I'll have to work.'

'And when you're not working and there's just the two of you alone in paradise? It sounds like this Tom Maddison is pretty hot,' said Amanda. 'How are you going to keep your hands off him? And don't tell me you haven't thought about it!'

'I haven't!' And she hadn't. Not since Tom had announced that he was getting married, anyway.

'Honestly, Amanda, the man has just been jilted at the altar,' Imogen went on a little huffily. 'He won't admit it, but he's really hurt. The last thing he needs is me making things awkward for him! Besides, this is my boss we're talking about.'

'So?'

'So there's no question of anything like that. Tom's too churned up about Julia and I've got more sense. OK, he is quite attractive,' Imogen conceded, 'but he's out of my league, I know that.

'Even if he wasn't in love with someone else, I wouldn't consider it,' she went on. 'Tom Maddison doesn't even have a nodding acquaintance with his emotions. Look at how he's suppressing everything now! A relationship with a man like him would be asking for trouble. I'd end up miserable, and I've had enough misery, thank you very much.

'Quite apart from anything else, it would be unprofessional,' Imogen finished primly. 'It's a well-paid job, and if I can stick it for another two or three months I'll have enough money to take off for a year. There's no way I'm risking that for the sake of a quick fling. No,' she told Amanda, 'I don't think I'll have any trouble keeping my hands to myself!'

Now her words rang a little hollowly in her ears. It had been easy to say in London. She had been so confident then, but that was before he had touched her, before the nerves beneath her skin had started jumping and jittering with awareness of him. Before that long flight, sitting right next to him.

They had travelled first-class, of course, and to Imogen, used to cheap package holidays, it had been absolute luxury. She had been thrilled, playing with her chair, opening her free bag of toiletries, accepting a glass of champagne.

Only she would have enjoyed it more if Amanda had been with her, say. Tom wasn't the kind of person you could have a giggle with.

Understandably enough, he was looking forbidding when he'd come to pick her up from her flat in a chauffeur-driven limousine that had whisked them out to Heathrow. Conversation so far had been confined to practicalities about passports and boarding times. There had been no speculation about what to buy in Duty Free, no testing of perfumes or loitering in the bookshops. The First Class Lounge was very comfortable, but it wasn't much fun, Imogen had decided.

Tom had sat down and opened his laptop and, apart from take-off and landing, he had worked steadily. To Imogen, it seemed as if the anger and hurt over Julia's rejection was still buttoned up tightly inside him. She desperately wanted to help him but she didn't know how. With anyone else she would offer a hug, but she hesitated even to lay a hand on Tom's arm.

Which was difficult when it was just *there*. Imogen could

see the immaculate cuff of his pale blue shirt, the expensive watch, the square, capable hand, and she'd found herself fixating on tiny details, like the creases on his knuckles, or the fine dark hairs at his wrist.

Afraid that Tom would see her staring, she'd forced herself to look at the magazine she had bought instead, but her eyes kept straying back to him. His gaze had been fixed on the computer screen and, with the piercing grey eyes shielded, it was easier to study his face. He had surprisingly thick, dark lashes, but the uncompromising angles of cheek and jaw offset any suggestion of softness, as did his mouth, which was set in a stern, straight line. Every time Imogen's eyes had come to rest on it, she got a squirmy, fluttery feeling inside.

In the end, it had been a relief to get off the plane and have something else to look at but, as Imogen sat in the boat, the reality of the situation began to sink in. She was about to spend three weeks alone with a man she found unsettlingly attractive, who just happened to be (a) her boss and (b) in love with someone else, and therefore doubly out of bounds.

Imogen adjusted her sunglasses and tried to wriggle the tension out of her shoulders. Perhaps Amanda was right and it was all going to be a terrible mistake.

But how could it be a mistake when the sun was warm on her skin, and the sea so clear that she could see every ripple in the sand beneath the boat? When she could hear the water slapping gently against the hull and smell the bleached wood of the jetty?

She could be in London, making the most of Tom's absence by catching up on her filing. She could be fielding phone calls and dealing with the emails stacked up in her inbox and chasing up those expenses with the Finance department.

Instead, she was here, with Tom, very distinct beside her, his austere profile outlined against the tropical sky. Eyeing him surreptitiously from behind her glasses, Imogen felt as if she had never seen him properly before. He had put on his sunglasses, which made his expression even more inscrutable than ever, but everything else about him seemed preternaturally clear in the light that bounced off the water: the texture of his skin, the line of his cheek, the faint stubble darkening his jaw after the long flight, the edge of his mouth.

She wished it would curl in a smile sometimes.

The boat started slowly, making its way out to the gap between the reef, but once on the open water the throbbing note of the engine deepened to a throaty roar as Ali accelerated and they skimmed over the waves.

The sun glittered on the water and, in spite of the windshield, Imogen's hair blew crazily around her face. It was so exhilarating that she could feel her fretfulness unravelling with every bounce of the boat and, without thinking, she smiled at Tom, who looked startled for a moment until, incredibly, he smiled back.

'OK?' he shouted over the noise of the engine, and she nodded vigorously as she tried to hold her hair back.

'It's wonderful!' she said, trying to ignore the breathless flip of her heart at his smile.

Although it had only taken a matter of minutes to reach the island in the powerful boat, it felt as if they had entered another world, one that made the laid-back resort seem a frenetic metropolis in comparison. When Ali cut the engine, the silence hit them like a blow.

'Welcome to Coconut Island,' he said.

From the little wooden jetty, Imogen could see the curve of a blindingly white beach, overhung with the coconut palms that cast a jagged shade. A lagoon the colour of a glacier mint and as clear as glass was encircled by a reef, but beyond that there was just the Indian Ocean, stretching out to a horizon smudged with a few billowing clouds. They had been promised seclusion, and seclusion they certainly had.

Set back from the beach and half hidden by a tangle of tropical foliage, from the outside the house was a simple wooden structure with a thatched roof, but inside it was furnished with exquisite style and discreetly fitted with latest technology from top designers.

The attention to detail made Imogen's jaw drop as Ali showed them round. Outside, there was an infinity pool, a Jacuzzi and a second fabulous bathroom open to the sky, with a wet area, a waterfall shower and a bath that would hold two easily, all perfectly designed in natural materials to blend into the foliage.

Inside, there was an immaculately equipped kitchen. There were polished wooden floors, inviting luxurious couches and low tables. There were revolving fans, and a sound system the like of which Imogen had never seen before.

And there was a very beautiful bed.

It had to be at least seven feet wide, and made with white sheets of the softest and purest cotton and piled with inviting pillows. A bed made for love.

Imogen, who had been exclaiming with pleasure as Ali showed them round, fell suddenly silent.

She glanced at Tom. His expression was unreadable, but she could imagine all too well what he must be thinking. How could he not be imagining in his turn what it would have been like if Julia had been there with him? If they had been impatient for Ali to leave them alone so that they could fall across that wonderful bed and make love?

It would be heaven. Imogen swallowed, unable to stop herself wondering what it would be like if she and Tom really were on honeymoon, if she was here because he loved her, not because Julia had left him in the lurch.

Too polite to comment on the awkward silence that had developed in the bedroom, Ali continued the tour, showing them the meals that had been left in the fridge, discussing the menu for the next day and pointing out the generator. Then he got into the speedboat and headed back to the resort, leaving Tom and Imogen alone.

They watched the boat speed out through the reef and then veer right in the direction of the islands they had passed on their way, its wake foaming behind it, and then even the sound of its engine vanished.

Imogen listened hard. She could hear the ocean murmuring against the reef, and somewhere a bird called raucously, but otherwise it was utterly quiet.

'Well,' she said awkwardly.

'Well,' agreed Tom in a dry voice.

Biting her lip, she looked out over the lagoon, which was achingly clear and green in the glaring light of midday. A cat's paw of breeze shivered over its surface and rustled the palms overhead, but then it was gone, leaving the scene still and dreamlike in the heat.

'Do you think you can spend three weeks here?' he asked her after a moment.

'Oh, yes, of course! It's absolutely *beautiful*,' she said. 'I feel as if I've stumbled into paradise! I just wish…'

Tom lifted an eyebrow as she hesitated. 'What?'

'I just wish things could be different for you,' she told him impulsively. 'I know how hard it must be for you to have me here instead of Julia.'

'Don't worry about it,' said Tom gruffly. 'I'm more afraid that you'll be bored.'

'Bored?' Imogen stared at him. 'How could I be bored *here*?' she asked, waving a hand at the view.

'You've always struck me as a very sociable person,' he explained to her surprise. She hadn't realised he had observed her at all. 'I see you chatting to people in the office and talking to your friends on the phone.'

Imogen grimaced at that bit. She had hoped Tom hadn't realised how much time she spent on personal phone calls.

'You seem like the kind of girl who likes to have fun,' he went on, uncharacteristically hesitant. 'There won't be much fun with just me for company.'

The truth was, he hadn't been thinking about Imogen. He had been so consumed with the bitterness of humiliation that he had thought only about getting away, and it was only now, very belatedly, that he was wondering if he had been selfish. Julia had often told him he needed to work on his social skills, but he had never been good at the kind of light-hearted conversation at which Imogen seemed to excel.

She made an unlikely PA, with that slightly chaotic air, but behind the warmth and the friendliness he had noted in her dealings with everyone from the most senior directors to the cleaners, she was unexpectedly practical, and Tom was grateful to her for the way she had dealt with the aftermath of Julia's change of mind. She deserved a better time than he would be able to give her.

Not that there was much he could do about it now. Tom hunched a shoulder. He hated feeling that he had got things wrong. He liked to be in control and know what was going on, and as soon as any emotions were involved, he was neither.

'You make it sound as if I'm a wild party animal,' said Imogen, amused but also secretly flattered. 'To be honest, I spend most evenings watching television with my flatmate and complaining about how nothing exciting ever happens to us. And now I'm here…' She looked around her. 'I couldn't ask for more exciting than this!'

Unless it was someone to share that beautiful bed with, a

sneaky voice in her mind had the temerity to point out before Imogen squashed it firmly.

'I promise you I'm more than happy just to look at this view for three weeks,' she told Tom. 'Of course, I'm happy to work too,' she added hastily, remembering their agreement.

'There's no need for you to work today,' said Tom gruffly. 'Since we're here, we may as well make the most of it.'

Imogen beamed at him. 'Sounds good to me.'

'So…what would you like to do? Are you tired?'

'A bit,' she confessed, 'but I want to swim first. I can't wait to get in that water!'

Ali had put their cases together in the bedroom. Tom's was sleek and black, Imogen's squashy and battered, and they sat side by side, looking bizarrely mismatched and yet oddly intimate at the same time.

Imogen fished out her bikini and changed in the en suite bathroom. Adjusting the straps, she regarded her reflection in the mirror dubiously. Had this bikini been *quite* so revealing the year before? It certainly didn't leave much to the imagination!

Why hadn't she stuck more carefully to that diet she had planned in January? If she had known she would be dusting off her bikini in February, she would never have eaten her way through all those packets of chocolate biscuits.

On the other hand, they were all that had got her through some of those long winter afternoons.

It was too late now, anyway. Imogen pulled herself together. Tom already had his laptop open, and when he was working he wouldn't notice if she walked past him stark naked. He certainly wouldn't be eyeing her up and wondering if a one-piece in a bigger size wouldn't have been a better choice, the way another woman would. There was a lot to be said for having a whole beach to yourself.

Still, she wrapped a sarong around her waist before heading out to the living area. Tom might not notice the way she spilled out of her bikini bottoms, but she would, and she didn't want to have to hold her tummy in all the time.

Tom was on one of the couches, leaning forward and frowning intently at the laptop open on the coffee table in front of him, but he looked up as Imogen appeared.

'Don't you want a swim?' she said, feeling self-conscious. He had barely glanced at her before returning his gaze to the screen, but it was enough to make her aware that the sarong was very thin and that, beneath it, she was practically naked.

'Maybe later,' he said. 'I want to check the markets first.'

'OK. Well….I'll be on the beach if you need me.'

When she had gone, Tom let out a long breath and slumped back against the cushions. He had been totally unprepared for the sight of Imogen, barefoot and wearing little more than a skimpy sarong. He recognised the brown hair tumbling to her shoulders, and the wide blue eyes, but had she always had that body? How had he never noticed before what luscious curves she had, or how lush and alluring her skin looked?

And now that he *had* noticed, how was he going to stop?

Tom scowled. He was still bruised from his last encounter with a woman, and he certainly didn't intend to get entangled with another, especially not one who was his PA. It would be totally inappropriate.

He shouldn't even be thinking about how she had looked. He certainly shouldn't be wondering if she would feel as soft and warm as she looked, wondering what it would be like to unwind that sarong and explore that unexpectedly voluptuous body with his mouth and his hands.

Setting his teeth grimly, Tom forced his attention back to the screen. He must be suffering some kind of a delayed reaction to the last few days, he decided. Nothing else could explain the lust that had gripped him when he had looked up to see Imogen just now. It wasn't even as if she was his type. He had never even thought about what she looked like before. His preference had always been for slender, sophisticated women—women who were cool and controlled. Women like Julia.

Julia. The thought of her was like a shock. Had it only been three days since he had been ready to marry her? Tom couldn't believe that he was thinking lustfully about another woman already. He had to stop it, right now, he thought. They had another three weeks to get through—three weeks when he would have to keep his hands firmly to himself.

He could do it. He could do whatever he set his mind to, Tom reminded himself. Hadn't he built an entire career on sheer willpower and determination, on a refusal to let himself be distracted from his goal? He had resisted a lot more tempting distractions than Imogen, and he would resist her too. Quite apart from anything else, he didn't want to distract *her*. They had work to do.

And work was what Tom Maddison did best.

It was hard to concentrate on it right then, though. He was hot and his eyes felt gritty from the plane. A quick dip would refresh him, Tom decided. An image of the lagoon shimmered in his mind, but he dismissed it. Imogen was down there. He didn't want to crowd her.

Odd how vividly he could picture her, he mused, remembering how she had looked, smiling on the boat, her hair tangled around her face and her eyes full of sunshine, how she had looked in that sarong with her shoulders bare.

Remembering that was a mistake.

Restlessly, Tom got to his feet and wandered outside. The infinity pool shimmered invitingly. He would cool off in there and then get back to work.

But the pool seemed empty somehow and when he hung in the water with his arms stretched along the edge he could see the lagoon through the palms and he found himself imagining Imogen down there, on her own.

Really, it was ridiculous to feel that he had to avoid her! They were going to have to get on together for the next three weeks.

It wasn't as if there was a problem, not really. Tom had already rationalised his momentary surge of lust as the simple reaction of a bruised ego. He might be alone on a tropical island with Imogen, but they were both sensible adults. There was absolutely no reason why they shouldn't have the same professional relationship they had always had, and get on with some work.

Work was what mattered.

Hauling himself out of the pool, Tom dried himself off and went into the kitchen. Imogen wouldn't be able to work if she was suffering from dehydration. He would take her a drink.

He found her stretched out on a lounger in the jagged shade of a palm. She had discarded the sarong somewhere along the line and was wearing only a bright pink bikini. Tom's hand wasn't quite steady as he offered her a glass of fresh lime juice.

'Thank you,' she said, sitting up, but her smile as she took the glass from him was definitely tense.

It couldn't be easy for her, stuck here with her boss, thought Tom.

He sat on the edge of the lounger set out beside hers and stared out at the lagoon while he sipped his own drink and willed the image of Imogen in that bikini to stop dancing before his eyes.

He could do this. It was just a matter of getting used to seeing his PA without her clothes on.

There was a strained silence.

'What's the water like?' Tom asked eventually, uncomfortably aware that his voice came out as a rasp, and he cleared his throat.

'Lovely.' Imogen drained her glass and put it down in the sand as she stood up. 'I was about to go back in for another swim,' she said, then hesitated. 'Why don't you come?'

It might be better to do something rather than sit here trying not to look at her, Tom decided. 'All right,' he said, getting to his feet.

They walked over the hot sand together and into the water. It was so clear they could see their feet in extraordinary detail as they waded past the shallows.

'It feels like silk against your skin, doesn't it?' said Imogen, trailing her fingers over the surface.

Tom wished she hadn't mentioned her skin. It was hard enough to keep his eyes off it as it was. As soon as it was deep enough, he dived into the water and swam in a fast crawl out towards the reef.

It felt good to stretch himself physically. It certainly felt less dangerous than standing close to Imogen wearing little more than a few triangles of cloth.

When he stopped at last, he shook the hair out of his eyes and trod water. Here, it had deepened to jade, but he could still see right down to the bottom, some way below. The sun was bouncing off the surface and fracturing the water into silvery patterns, and he had to squint against the glare to find Imogen, who was floating dreamily on her back, legs and arms stretched out like a starfish.

It was very quiet. How long was it since he had stopped like this and just listened to the silence, just felt the sun on his shoulders? His life was so focused, so driven by the need to succeed that he had forgotten how to relax the way Imogen was relaxing. Maybe he had never known how to relax like that, thought Tom, but he had the strangest idea that the tight feeling that had gripped him for as long as he could remember was starting to loosen in the sunlight and the warm silky water.

CHAPTER FOUR

HE SWAM more slowly back to shore. By the time he got there, Imogen was lolling in the shallows. Leaning back on her hands, her head was tipped back as she lifted her face to the sun, but she opened her eyes at the sound of his approach.

'It's incredible, isn't it?' she said naturally enough, but there was still that constraint in her expression and her smile was guarded.

Tom knew how she felt. Imogen was his PA; he was her boss. It wasn't as if they were strangers, but it occurred to him—very belatedly—that they had never had what could properly be called a conversation and now he wasn't sure where to start. They had only ever talked about work, about practicalities, but they could hardly discuss either here, with the light rocking over the water and the hot breeze ruffling the palms.

The situation was more awkward than he had anticipated. The truth was that he had been so desperate to get away from the humiliation of a cancelled wedding that he hadn't really thought what it would be like being alone with Imogen. He had imagined that there would be plenty of room for both of them on the island and, although there obviously was, he could hardly walk past her and ignore her, could he?

After a moment's hesitation, he sat down next to her in the

shallows. He would try and avoid her as much as possible, but they were still going to have to establish some kind of relationship for the next three weeks. They couldn't spend their time together in silence. For now he had better try and make a bit of an effort.

Only it was harder than he thought when he was sitting right beside her. He had been careful not to get too close, but he was quite near enough to see how the wet bikini clung to Imogen's breasts.

Near enough to see the droplets of water on her skin and the curve of her mouth.

Near enough to see the sweep of her lashes, the pulse beating in her throat.

Tom cleared his throat and made himself look away. 'The water's very nice,' he agreed.

Imogen dug her toes into the sand and marvelled at his innocuous choice of words. It was more than *nice*. It was magical.

Dazzled by the heat and the light and the colour, she felt as if she had stumbled into another world and she had been sitting very still, half afraid that if she moved it would disappear in a blink and she would find herself back on the Northern Line, battling her way up into the greyness and the rain with the other commuters.

It was all so perfect, the blues and the greens and the pure white beach behind her. The colours were clean and clear and the only sound was the ocean, muted beyond the reef, and the gentle ripple of the lagoon around her ankles.

The only jarring note was Tom. He belonged in the other grey day-to-day world, not in this colourful idyllic one.

Imogen slid a sideways glance at him under her lashes. He was looking out towards the reef, his arms resting casually on his knees, and he seemed at once startlingly familiar and a stranger.

The stern profile, the dark formidable features, the close-cropped hair were the same as ever, but she wasn't used to seeing them etched against a perfect blue sky.

Or on top of a bare chest.

She had known that he was tall and lean, and she had assumed that he would have a decent body, but Imogen hadn't realised quite how good until he had appeared by the lounger wearing only those swimming shorts. It had been impossible not to notice that his legs were long and straight, his chest broad and wonderfully solid-looking, with dark hairs arrowing down to an enviably flat, hard stomach. He had powerful shoulders too, and his skin looked tantalisingly wet and touchable.

Imogen's mouth dried. She was desperately aware of him sitting in the water beside her. Normally she had no problem chatting to anyone, but Tom was hard work at the best of times and now that he was practically naked she couldn't think of a single thing to say.

The next three weeks were going to be awkward if she was going to feel stupidly shy like this the whole time. She wanted to treat Tom exactly the same as always, but how could she when he was sitting there with that body? She wished he would go and put his suit back on. It might not be very practical for the beach, but at least she would feel as if she knew where she was.

The silence lengthened uncomfortably. Imogen was still searching desperately for a neutral topic of conversation when a flash of light beneath the water caught her eye and she leant forward to see another, and then another. 'Look!' she cried, pointing at the tiny fish that darted over the sand and heartily relieved at the distraction. 'Aren't they beautiful?'

'There'll be a lot more out there.' Tom seized gratefully on the conversational gambit. Narrowing his eyes against the glare, he nodded towards the reef. 'I hear the snorkelling is spectacular.'

'I'd love to do that,' she said wistfully.

'You could get out there easily enough. I noticed a boat earlier.'

Imogen looked doubtful. 'I wouldn't know one end of a boat from another. I think I'd be better off swimming! Is snorkelling easy? I've never done it before.'

'I'll teach you if you like,' said Tom, who only moments before had decided that the only way to get through three weeks of Imogen in a bikini was to go their separate ways as much as possible.

'Really?'

So much for keeping his distance! Tom cursed himself for a fool. He couldn't have found a surer way to get close to her in that damned bikini if he'd tried. He was supposed to be getting back to a work relationship, not fooling around in the water.

'We'll have a go tomorrow. After we've done some work,' he added.

'I'd like that,' said Imogen, brightening. Perhaps it would be easier if they did something together. At least then they would have something to talk about.

She leant back on her elbows and looked at him curiously. There was little money in snorkelling, few deals to be negotiated on a coral reef. It seemed an unlikely activity for Tom to take part in. 'Where did you learn to snorkel?'

'In the Caribbean. I had a girlfriend once who went on and on about having a holiday together,' Tom remembered. 'I only went to shut her up, but it wasn't a success. We'd got on fine in London, but I suppose the truth was that we hadn't seen that much of each other. As soon as we got out there, we realised that we had nothing to say to each other. She lay on the beach and I went snorkelling, and once we got back to London I never saw her again!'

Imogen spread her hands, sliding them beneath the silvery sand. 'They say holidays are a real test of a relationship.'

'It certainly was for Helena and I, although according to Helena it was all my fault. She complained I didn't know how to relax, and there's some truth in that. I never know what to do with myself on holiday. I don't think I ever learnt. We never had holidays when we were growing up.'

'What, never?'

'Not the kind of holiday where you go away somewhere different, anyway. I had school holidays, of course, but my mother died when I was small and my father was always working, so I was pretty much left to my own devices.'

'Poor little boy,' said Imogen, but he shrugged off her sympathy.

'I liked it. I started my first business at the age of ten. I used to knock on neighbours' doors and offer to wash cars for a quid, until I realised that I was undercharging!' He smiled wryly at the memory.

'What did you do with your earnings?' she asked, intrigued by the idea of him as a little boy.

'I bought some extra buckets and some more cloths, and gave them to friends in exchange for a percentage of their earnings. By the end of the summer, I had quite a team!'

Imogen laughed. She was feeling better now that they were actually having a conversation. Perhaps this wouldn't be so bad after all. 'It sounds like you were always an entrepreneur!'

'I learnt early on that if I wanted anything, I had to get it for myself,' said Tom. 'Even at ten I could work out the laws of supply and demand. To get what I wanted, I needed money, but to get money all I had to do was work out what everyone else wanted and then make it easy for them to have it.'

'You make it sound so simple,' said Imogen with a touch of bitterness, and he raised his brows.

'It is simple.'

'Working out what people want? Not in my experience!'

He shrugged. 'I never had any trouble knowing what I wanted. It seems to me a lot of people don't *know* what they want. Once you do, you've got a clear objective, and then it's just a matter of working towards it. All you need is a strategy and be prepared to stick with it.'

'That might work in business, but strategies are no use when emotions are involved.'

'No.' Tom thought about Julia and how messy everything had become once he had forgotten just that. 'That's why I stick to business as much as possible. Whenever I venture into emotional territory, it turns into a disaster.'

He hadn't meant to sound bitter, but Imogen shot him a quick glance of concern.

'I'm sorry,' she said. 'I didn't mean to remind you of Julia. I was thinking of myself.'

'Oh?' Tom was glad to turn the conversation away from his inadequacies on the emotional front.

'I always knew what I wanted too, but much good it did me.'

'What *did* you want?'

Imogen sighed and clasped her arms around her knees. 'I wanted my boyfriend to love me again, that was all. I even had a strategy, as you call it. I was going to give him time, and then he'd realise that he missed me.'

'And he didn't?'

'No,' she said. 'He married someone else.'

Tom studied her profile. She had pushed her wet hair behind her ears and she was staring out to the horizon, lost in memories.

'There's no point in wanting something that depends on someone else,' he said after a moment. 'You can only succeed if you want things that you can achieve by yourself.'

Something he should have remembered before he'd asked Julia to marry him.

'But what if what you want is not to be by yourself?' asked Imogen, turning her head to look at him, and Tom found himself trapped by the directness of her gaze.

Had her eyes always been that blue? he wondered, almost startled by the depth of colour. Surely he would have noticed them before if they had?

It must be just the sea and the sky making them look so blue, he decided. A trick of the light.

'Then you probably won't succeed,' he said.

'Success isn't everything,' she pointed out.

'It is to me.'

Imogen didn't answer directly. To Tom's secret relief, she looked away once more to where the ocean surged and sighed beyond the reef.

'I remember in my last year at school, an older girl came to give us a talk,' she said eventually. 'I thought it was going to be really boring. She was a high-flying lawyer, very glamorous, and she seemed to have everything. We were all expecting her to tell us how we had to work hard to succeed, but she said something completely different.

'I've never forgotten,' Imogen remembered. 'She told us that the most important lesson we had to learn was how to fail. She said that we all fail at some time in our lives, and that what counted was not how much money we earned or how much status we had, but how we responded to failure. It was a test of character, she said. Did we let ourselves be beaten, or did we pick ourselves up and start again?'

Tom frowned. He had never let himself consider failure at all.

'And you bought this?'

'Well, it was very uplifting at the time,' said Imogen, almost apologetically. 'Especially for those of us who were more used to failing than succeeding. But I've got plenty of experience of failure now. I have to admit it would be nice to try success some time for a change!'

Tom was still brooding over the idea of failure. 'If you set yourself clear goals, there's no reason not to succeed,' he said.

'That depends on your goals, doesn't it? You can't make someone else love you,' she said a little sadly. 'You can't control how other people will react. If you're going to have any kind of relationship at all, you have to accept that you're not always going to succeed. There's no other option.'

'Unless you give up on relationships altogether.'

'But that's a failure too, isn't it?' said Imogen.

Her words seemed to reverberate over the shimmering lagoon. *Failure…failure…failure…*

Tom stirred uneasily. He wasn't used to failure. He didn't like it. He didn't know what to do with it.

But he had to face it. His relationship with Julia had been a failure. He knew it. Imogen knew it. Everyone knew it.

Humiliation burned in the pit of his stomach and he glared out at the horizon, his shoulders tense and hunched.

'So what did you learn from not getting your boyfriend back?'

Imogen didn't appear to notice the harshness in his voice. 'I learned that I don't want to compromise,' she said. 'I've accepted that Andrew doesn't love me any more. My friends have been telling me that I should get out there again and meet someone else, so I've been trying. I go out on dates, and I really do try to be positive, but I haven't met anyone who could even begin to make me feel the way I felt about Andrew. Every date feels like yet another failure now, so I've decided to stop looking.'

'You're giving up on men?'

'No. I'm giving up thinking that I might settle for something less than perfect.'

There was another long silence, broken only by the rippling of the lagoon and the faint sough of the wind in the coconut palms and, from somewhere in the island, the harsh screech of a bird.

Tom was thinking about what Imogen had said. Julia had tried to settle, he realised. He had only ever been second-best for her. The thought was bitter. Julia had made the right decision in the end, but it had left him feeling a failure.

That was how Imogen said she felt after every disastrous date. Funny, he had never thought of her as having a life of her own before. She had just been a PA and now…

Tom glanced at her. Her eyes were on the horizon, her expression dreamy or perhaps just wistful. She wasn't classically beautiful, like Julia, but there was something appealing about her. Tom couldn't put his finger on it. It might be that lovely lush skin, or the generous curve to her mouth, or perhaps the blueness and brightness of her eyes.

Now…now she was more than just a PA. Tom didn't know exactly what she was, but she was more than that.

Almost as if she could hear him thinking, Imogen turned her head to find him watching her and, as her clear, lovely blue eyes looked into his, Tom found himself struggling to breathe normally.

This was ridiculous, he told himself crossly. It was only Imogen.

'You're getting burnt.' He said the first thing that came into his mind, and touched a finger to her shoulder where her skin was pink. 'Sorry,' he said as she flinched.

Imogen swallowed. 'It's just a bit sore,' she said, not wanting to admit how aware she was of his touch. 'You're right, I'd better go into the shade for a while.'

Clambering inelegantly to her feet, she brushed the sand from her legs and pretended not to notice as Tom straightened beside her. Suddenly, he seemed very close, his chest broad, his shoulders powerfully muscled, his hips lean in the plain swimming shorts he wore, and her mouth dried.

'I might have a snooze,' she said, stepping back as if it would help her suck more oxygen into her lungs. 'It's all catching up with me now.'

'Why don't you go to bed for a couple of hours?'

Imogen managed to shake her head. She would never be able to relax in that bed, imagining what it would be like if things were different, if she could stretch out and wait for Tom to join her underneath that fine sheet, if he were to pull off those shorts and let her run her hands over that smooth, muscled body…

With some difficulty, she wrenched her mind away. 'I like it down here,' she said.

'Up to you.' Tom shrugged, plainly unbothered. 'I'll see you later, in that case.'

Imogen's body was buzzing with a mixture of exhaustion and a prickly awareness, so she didn't really expect to sleep when she lay on the lounger in the deep shade, but tiredness rolled over her like a wave the moment she closed her eyes, and when she opened them again it was to discover that it was nearly two hours later.

Groggily, she got to her feet, still squinting at her watch in case she had made a mistake, but the lengthening shadows told their own story. It looked as if she had had that snooze after all.

Vaguely aware of a lingering embarrassment, without really remembering why, Imogen made her way back to the house. The sun was low on the horizon and the sea lay flat and still while in the undergrowth unseen insects were warming up for a rasping, sawing, shrilling concert to mark the end of the day.

Tom had moved his laptop to the dining table and she could

see him studying the screen intently. How many times had she seen him wear exactly that focused expression? Imogen wondered. The line between his brows, the pugnacious set of his jaw, the stern line of his mouth…they were all completely familiar to her after working with him for the last few months.

So why did the sight of him feel like a fist colliding with her stomach, driving the air out of her lungs and leaving her jolted and jarred with the sudden shock of it?

It must be the jet lag catching up on her, Imogen decided, and drew a steadying breath as she put a foot on the veranda steps.

Tom looked up when she appeared in the doorway.

'That was a long snooze.'

'I didn't mean to sleep that long.' Imogen was glad to see he had put on a shirt and shorts. He looked cool and comfortable while she felt hot and drowsy and crumpled after her sleep. At least discomfort helped her shake aside that odd feeling of shocking familiarity.

'I think I'll have a shower,' she said. 'I'm still feeling a bit dopey.'

'You look it.'

His voice was cool, his glance faintly disapproving, and Imogen let out a breath she hadn't realised she'd been holding. It was a relief to realise that he was once more Tom, her irascible boss, a man impatient of weakness or frivolity.

So they had chatted in the shallows for a bit? What else were they supposed to do when they were all alone on a tropical island? Tom might have told her more about himself than she had ever known before, but he had just been making conversation and that wasn't the same as being intimate, no matter what it had felt like.

She certainly wasn't going to start being silly just because she had seen what a good body lurked beneath those suits he always wore. It had just been tiredness making her uncomfortably aware of him as a man rather than a boss, Imogen told herself. She would just have a cool shower and change into something sensible, and they would be back to their normal professional relationship in no time.

The light was fading rapidly as she made her way out to the bathroom. It was open to the sky and the subdued lights made the curving walls and clever tiling look wonderfully romantic. The lack of a door made Imogen a little uncomfortable, but Tom knew where she was, she reasoned. He was hardly likely to come barging in on her and, with no one else on the island, she could hardly ask for more privacy.

She turned her attention to the shower, peering at the controls in the dim light. There were no screens, no panels, just an enormous shower head that stuck out over the tiled floor that sloped slightly to drain. It would be like standing under a waterfall.

Imogen's skin was hot and gritty, and her hair was full of sand. It was going to be wonderful, she told herself as she turned the controls and pulled off her bikini.

With a sigh of relief, she stepped under the cascade of water, only to feel something scuttle horribly underfoot. Something she hadn't seen in the stupid lighting, which was suddenly not romantic at all, but downright dangerous.

Something that had a friend to scrabble over her foot as she jerked it away.

Imogen couldn't help herself. She screamed and leapt out of the water, bolting to the other side of the bathroom without even stopping to grab a towel.

The next moment Tom came skidding round the curving bathroom wall. 'What's the ma—oh!'

He stopped dead at the realisation that Imogen was stark naked.

Imogen's heart was galloping with a mixture of fright and the sheer shock of seeing Tom charge into the room, but for a long, excruciating moment she could only stare back at him from behind the Jacuzzi.

He wondered if she had any idea how she looked, with her hair damp and her skin wet and her eyes wide and dark with fright. Her hand was pressed to her throat where a pulse jumped wildly, and her breasts were rising and falling rapidly as she struggled for breath.

That bikini hadn't left much to the imagination, but Tom was still unprepared for the glorious lushness of her body, and even though his brain was yelling at him to keep his eyes firmly on her face while he backed out, it didn't stand a chance against the pull of instinct which dropped his gaze to skim over those lovely curves.

Imogen saw his eyes drop and, far too late, humiliation jerked her out of her paralysis.

'God, I'm sorry,' Tom managed as she snatched at a towel.

Of course it was far too small, and she had to hold it ridiculously in front of her while she pulled at one that looked big enough to wrap round her, her cheeks burning with embarrassment.

'I heard you scream,' he tried to explain, backing out. 'I thought something was wrong.'

'I trod on something when I got in the shower.' Imogen shuddered at the memory. 'You can't see a thing in this stupid light,' she complained, forgetting how she had gasped at how pretty the room looked at first. 'It was revolting.'

'What was it?' Tom had his voice under better control. At least she was covered by the towel now, not that it made that much difference. The image of her body was still vivid after he had stared like a grubby schoolboy. He shifted his shoulders uncomfortably, mortified by the memory.

'I don't know,' said Imogen. 'I didn't stop to inspect it. It felt disgusting, whatever it was.'

Tom went over to turn the shower off. It gave him a good excuse to look away from Imogen, if nothing else. 'Probably a cockroach,' he said. 'Yes, there he is.' He pointed at the corner, where something dark and shiny lurked, antennae waving malevolently.

Imogen peered nervously round Tom's shoulder. 'Ugh! It's horrible!'

'It probably doesn't think too much of you either after you trod on it.' Tom was finding it hard to concentrate with her so close to him. 'Do you want me to get rid of it for you?'

'Would you?' said Imogen gratefully. She had been wondering how to ask him to do just that without sounding pathetic.

Tom stepped towards the cockroach but it was too quick for him. It dashed for the other wall, and its sudden scuttle made Imogen squeak and jump back. The movement loosened the wretched towel, which promptly started to unwind.

'Oh—!' Imogen only just managed to bite back a curse as she grabbed the towel in the nick of time.

Fortunately Tom didn't notice. He was too busy following the cockroach around the bathroom, but the faster he stamped, the quicker the insect moved and the more he missed. He muttered furiously under his breath as his shoes rang uselessly on the tiled floor. No cockroach was going to get the better of Tom Maddison!

He looked so ridiculous, stamping around the shower in frustration, and the situation was so bizarre, that Imogen's sense of humour began to get the better of her. It might have been tiredness, or an edge of hysteria, but she could feel laughter bubbling up inside her.

'Gosh,' she said, 'I didn't know you could do flamenco.'

Distracted, Tom stopped in mid-stamp. 'What?'

'A ruthless businessman *and* a hot dancer.' Imogen's expression was innocent as she nodded at his feet. 'You've got to admit, it's quite a combination!'

For a moment Tom could only stare at her. The light was dim but it was enough to see the mischief glimmering in her eyes. A smile was tugging at the corners of her mouth, and all at once he realised how comical he must look, chasing an insect around the shower, watched by his PA, who was utterly naked beneath that skimpy towel.

Did anyone enjoy looking stupid? Tom certainly never had before but, in spite of his exasperation, he felt an answering smile twitch his lips. What an absurd situation to find himself in, but perhaps it was a fitting ending for what should have been his wedding day. It might have started in tragedy, but it was ending in farce.

Without thinking, he lifted his arms, snapped his fingers and stamped his heel dramatically. *'Olé!'* he cried, striking a pose.

It was Imogen's turn to stare, startled by his uncharacteristic lapse into absurdity, and then they both started to laugh at the same time.

They laughed and they laughed, until they were both almost doubled up. It wasn't that funny, but at some level both were aware that their laughter came as much from the release from some unspoken tension as from the humour of the situation.

'Oh dear,' gasped Imogen at last, mopping her eyes with the edge of the towel. 'I think I needed that!'

'And, after all of that, the cockroach has legged it,' Tom realised, looking around the room, as Imogen started to giggle again.

He was feeling a bit odd. He couldn't remember the last time he had laughed like that—laughed *uncontrollably*. Usually, the whole notion of being out of control made him uncomfortable, but now, when he looked at Imogen, it wasn't the scariness of losing control he was thinking about.

It was Imogen's face, still alight with laughter.

It was Imogen's body, beneath the towel that kept slipping dangerously.

He should go before she lost grip of it completely, Tom decided.

'You can have that shower now,' he told her, and then cocked an eyebrow at her hesitation. 'Unless you'd prefer to use the one inside?'

'I would, of course, but then you would think that I'm really pathetic.'

'What, because you're afraid of a little cockroach? Never!'

Imogen made a face at him. 'See, I knew you'd say that! If I went to the other bathroom, I'd never be able to hold up my head again.'

'I won't say another word,' promised Tom, holding up his hands.

'No, no, I'm determined to shower here now. I'm a big, brave girl now, especially as I know that all it takes to see off a cockroach is a bit of bad dancing!'

He smiled as he turned to leave. 'I'll leave you to it then. Scream if you need me.'

She wouldn't be screaming again, but she needed him, all right. She needed him to go back to being her brusque, irritable boss, thought Imogen, dropping the towel and stretching out her hand to test the temperature of the water. She needed him to stop smiling like that. She needed him to put his suit back on and make her forget that he had that great body.

Imogen had looked forward to the shower, but as she stood under the cascade of warm water she found herself thinking, not about how good it felt to wash the sun and the salt out of her hair but about Tom, and how he had laughed.

Who would have thought that the coolly calculating Tom Maddison would play the fool like that? Imogen smiled as she remembered him striking that flamenco dancer's pose and shouting *olé*! He might have been a different man entirely from the one who barked instructions down the phone or wished her a curt good morning as he strode through her office in London.

This Tom had an unexpectedly wide smile with good teeth, and when he had thrown back his head and laughed, his eyes had creased and the harsh lines of his face had been transformed by amusement. Imogen felt something disturbing start to uncoil inside her at the mere memory, and she shivered uneasily.

The truth was that she was more afraid of that feeling than of the cockroach coming back.

And there was no point going there, she reminded herself sternly. This should have been Tom's wedding day, remember? It should have been Julia standing here, feeling her skin tingle with that heady mixture of sea water and slightly too much sun.

Imogen was fairly sure that Julia wouldn't have screamed at the sight of a cockroach. Or, if she had, she wouldn't have stood there stark naked while those glacial grey eyes swept over her.

But then, of course, Julia would be used to Tom looking at her, Imogen reflected glumly as she dressed. In fact, Julia wouldn't have been showering alone, would she? Tom would have been in there with her, and they would have been too busy making love under that glorious cascade of water to notice a whole parade of cockroaches.

Imogen's cheeks burned at the thought. How awful for Tom to see her instead of Julia at every turn, to have come face to face with his naked PA, whose body could most kindly be described as curvaceous, instead of Julia's slender, perfect beauty. It must have been a horrible shock for him.

Still, she was glad that they had been able to laugh together like that. It felt as if everything had changed now. At least the awkwardness of finding themselves alone together had passed. Of course, there could be few things more embarrassing than your boss catching you stark naked, but there was no point in being shy after that, Imogen decided philosophically. The change in the atmosphere was worth the humiliation.

CHAPTER FIVE

IMOGEN felt quite positive as she dressed, in spite of knowing that her pale aqua sundress was a far cry from the perfect sexy, stylish outfit that Julia would inevitably have had to slip into after her shower. But it would just have to do. OK, so it looked cheap and a little crumpled in these luxurious surroundings, but it might not be a bad thing to have a reminder that she could loll all she wanted in the lagoon but she would always be out of place in these fabulous surroundings.

It wouldn't do to start thinking that the fact that she was here with Tom was anything other than a face-saving measure. He was a successful businessman; she was a temp. He took this kind of designer luxury for granted; her style was cheap, cheery and chain-store. It would be very foolish of her to forget that.

On the other hand, since she was here, she might as well make the best of it. Now they had broken the tension with laughter, perhaps they could at least be friends for the next three weeks. She was never going to replace the svelte, sophisticated Julia, but she could be a friend, even if it was only a temporary one.

Temporary secretary, temporary friend… When would she ever settle to anything permanent? Imogen wondered wistfully.

Not until she was sure that what she had was perfect, she reminded herself firmly.

In the meantime, she was in the middle of the Indian Ocean, on an idyllic island with a man who needed a friend right now. That would be enough, she told herself.

An image of Tom in his swimming shorts flickered distractingly in her brain, but Imogen forced her mind away from thoughts of that lean, tautly muscled body.

Away from the image of his hands.

Of his mouth.

From the memory of how he had looked when he was laughing.

Friends would be enough for now.

Slipping her feet into her favourite sequinned flip-flops, Imogen went out to find Tom.

He was waiting for her on the veranda, his feet up on the railing and a beer in his hand, looking more relaxed than she had ever seen him.

'Better?' he asked as he saw her.

'Much, thank you.'

Tom swung his legs down. 'Would you like a drink?'

He made her a gin and tonic. It was deliciously cold and refreshing, and Imogen sipped it appreciatively as she leant against the railing.

It looked as if she had missed a glorious sunset while she was in the shower. She could see through the coconut palms to where the lagoon gleamed dark and still, and beyond to a vivid streak of crimson along the horizon. Unseen insects were working themselves up into a frenzy of creaking and whirring and sawing and rasping in the tangled foliage, and the air was hot and heavy with the intense scents of the tropical night.

Suddenly something swooped in front of her, and she straightened in surprise. 'Was that a bird?'

'A bat, I think.'

Imogen wrinkled her nose. 'First cockroaches, now bats…
Somehow this isn't how I imagined paradise!' she said dryly
as she watched the creatures, darting and diving through the
hot dark air.

'Don't tell me you're afraid of bats too?'

'Of course not,' she said, shooting him a look. 'I'm not
afraid of cockroaches either,' she said, not entirely truthfully.
'I know I screamed, but it was just a shock seeing it there. I
wasn't expecting it,' she finished lamely.

Tom looked down at his beer and reflected that he knew
how she had felt. He hadn't been expecting to see her without
any clothes on either, and that had been just as much of a
shock, if in a different way.

'About earlier,' he said abruptly. 'I'm sorry if I embarrassed you, bursting in like that.'

'That's OK. I'm glad you were there. I would never have
been able to scare that cockroach away by myself.' Her smile
glimmered. 'My flamenco dancing isn't up to much!'

The corner of Tom's mouth lifted at the reminder of what
had set them laughing. He was glad Imogen had mentioned
it. When she had appeared, looking lush and glowing after her
shower, her hair falling damply to her shoulders, he had
wondered if the idea that had come to him while she was
showering might be asking for trouble, but now the constraint
had eased he decided to put it to her after all.

'I've been thinking,' he began.

'Oh?'

He gestured around him. 'This place…it's much more
intimate than I was expecting.'

'It's meant for honeymooners,' Imogen pointed out. 'It
would be surprising if it *wasn't* intimate.'

'I know,' said Tom with just a touch of his old irritability.
'I wasn't thinking clearly.'

'That's understandable,' she said, instantly feeling guilty. 'None of this can be easy for you.'

'The thing is…' Tom frowned, wondering how best to put it. 'We've got three weeks here,' he began again. 'The chances are that we're going to find ourselves in more embarrassing situations when there's just the two of us.

'I thought with it being a whole island we'd have more space,' he tried to explain himself. It had all seemed so obvious when he was working it out in his mind, but it felt more difficult with Imogen's eyes on his face. He was no good at this kind of stuff. If he wasn't careful, he'd be talking about his feelings.

'As it is, we're going to be effectively living together for the next three weeks,' he ploughed on. 'That's going to be awkward unless we agree to be…I don't know…*normal*.'

'That's just what I was thinking,' said Imogen eagerly.

'I'm just not quite sure what normal is,' confessed Tom.

'Let's be friends. Just temporary ones, of course,' she added quickly in case he thought she was trying to take advantage of Julia's departure.

'Temporary?'

'Well, it would be difficult to go back to working together if we were friends, wouldn't it?'

'Perhaps,' he acknowledged. There was no use pretending it wouldn't be awkward, anyway.

'But, in any case, I'm leaving soon,' Imogen went on, 'so I won't be around much longer.'

'Leaving?' Tom asked, startled. 'Why?'

'I'm going to travel,' she said. 'I've never been outside Europe before. I've always wanted to go to India, so I'm going to start there and make my way down through South-East Asia to Australia, and I hope that on the way I'll decide what it is I really want to do with my life.'

Now that she had finally given up dreaming of Andrew.

Tom was frowning. 'I didn't know about this.'

'That's why I'm temping,' said Imogen. 'Didn't you know? I'm only filling in until you appoint a properly qualified executive PA.'

He *had* known that, of course. He just hadn't wanted to think about it. He had been too busy steering Collocom away from the rocks to take the time to choose the right person. Besides, Imogen might not be your classically cool and competent secretary, but she had been managing well enough. There had been no reason to think about replacing her.

'When's all this going to happen?' asked Tom, conscious of an uneasy feeling in the pit of his stomach. That wasn't *dismay*, was it?

'As soon as you appoint a permanent PA. I've been saving for nearly a year now, so I'm ready to book my ticket whenever you find the right person. I assumed you were putting it off until after the wedding, but if you interview in April and we have a handover in May, I could be packing my bags in June.'

'*June?*' No mistaking the dismay now! 'That's only three months away!'

Imogen nodded. 'I know, but if it's awkward when we get back, well, at least it won't be for long.'

Tom looked out into the night and tried to imagine the office without Imogen. Oh, he'd known she would go one day, but he hadn't thought it would be so soon. She was as much part of his life as Julia had been, if not more so. He saw Imogen almost every day, after all. It would be strange without her now.

But it wouldn't be the first time he had had to get used to a new PA, Tom reminded himself, alarmed by the bleak drift of his thoughts. He would be fine.

'That might work out quite well then,' he said, conscious that he sounded as if he were trying to convince himself.

'You're right, it might be difficult to go back to our old boss/PA relationship after being here, but if you're leaving soon, that won't matter.'

'Exactly,' said Imogen, keeping her smile bright.

What had she expected? That Tom would fall to his knees and beg her not to leave him?

No, it would be better this way. There was bound to be speculation at the office when they went back. The sooner she left and got on with her new life, the better, but for now, being friends, even temporary ones, seemed like the best way to get through the next three weeks.

'So are we agreed?' she said. 'As long as we're here, we're not boss and PA any more, but just friends?'

There was only the tiniest moment of hesitation, then Tom nodded. 'Agreed.'

'Great,' said Imogen. 'Now that's settled, let's go and see what's for supper. I'm starving!'

She chatted easily as she set out the delicacies that had been left in the fridge, and Tom found himself almost mesmerised by the readiness with which she was prepared to treat him as a friend. It made him realise how little he had known about her when she was just his PA. He had had no idea that she could be that sharp or that funny, and he watched her as if he had never seen her before as she told him about her friends, about the flat she shared with her friend and the life she led in London, so different from his own.

Suddenly Imogen broke off with a grimace as she listened to her own words. 'This must all sound so dull to you!' she said.

'Actually, it doesn't,' said Tom, almost to his own surprise. They had found a bottle of perfectly chilled wine in the fridge, and he leant across the table to top up her glass.

Imogen didn't believe him, of course. What had she been thinking of, rabbiting on about wine bars and chaotic supper parties and the snap quizzes she and Amanda held to test their embarrassingly wide knowledge of TV soaps? She cringed at the memory.

'But your life is so much more glamorous!'

She couldn't imagine Tom sprawled in front of the television, for instance. He and Julia would have gone out to smart restaurants or grand parties. They would have been to the opera or polo matches or the kind of clubs she and Amanda only ever read about in magazines.

'Is it?' said Tom. 'My apartment may be bigger than yours, and I may live in a more exclusive part of town, but I don't do much when I'm there. I just work.'

'What about when you were with Julia?'

He shrugged. 'We'd eat out a lot, and yes, there would quite often be some kind of reception, but those events aren't nearly as much fun as they're cracked up to be.'

What *had* he and Julia done together? Tom tried to remember. Julia was into art, but galleries and openings bored him rigid. He had often used work as an excuse not to go with her. Perhaps Patrick had gone instead?

It was all obvious in hindsight, of course, but shouldn't he have wondered how much he and Julia had in common before he'd asked her to marry him? He had thought that a similarly cool and careful approach to life would be enough. How wrong could you be?

He looked across the table at Imogen, whose own approach to life could by no stretch of the imagination be described as cool and careful, certainly not from what she'd been telling him.

'I don't think you'd enjoy my life that much,' he told her. 'It sounds as if you like the one you've got. You've got lots of friends, you seem to have a good time. You've got a job. Why give that up and leave your life behind to travel?'

'Because I need to get away,' said Imogen, her expression uncharacteristically serious.

Resting her arms on the table, she turned the glass pensively between her fingers. 'I spent five years holding on to an impossible dream,' she went on after a moment. 'Five years wanting something I couldn't have. I've finally accepted that it's not going to happen, but I think I need a complete break to do something completely different before I can move on properly.'

'Five years is a long time to want something—or was it some*one*?'

'Someone.' Imogen nodded.

Tom thought about what she had told him on the beach and searched his memory for a name. 'Andrew?'

'Andrew,' she confirmed. 'We were students together,' she told Tom. 'I fell in love with him the moment I laid eyes on him in Freshers' Week and we were inseparable for three years.

'I was so happy all that time,' she remembered, her smile tinged with sadness. 'It never occurred to me that it would end. I just assumed that, once we graduated, we'd get married and spend the rest of our lives together.'

'So what happened?' asked Tom.

'Oh, nothing dramatic. Andrew just…grew out of me.' Imogen managed a smile, but it was a painful one. 'After all, we were very young when we met, just eighteen, and only twenty-one when we graduated. People kept asking me what I wanted to do, meaning that I should be thinking about a career, but all I wanted to do was be with Andrew. He was more ambitious. He wanted to be a journalist, and that's what he did. He's doing well, too. He's just been made education correspondent on one of the national papers.'

'And you didn't blend with his décor any more, was that it?'

'No, not really.' It was second nature for Imogen to defend

Andrew now. 'Andrew realised that we wanted different things out of life. I was always happy to live in the moment, but he's a planner and thinks about the future in a way I never did. I think he was feeling stifled too, although he didn't put it like that.'

'How *did* he put it?'

'He said he thought we both needed a bit of space. We'd been living together for three years, after all, and neither of us had ever really spent any time on our own. He thought we should have a chance to meet other people before we settled down, and he was right. Twenty-one is much too young to tie yourself down for life—although I didn't think so at the time, of course,' she added with a wry smile.

Tom was trying to imagine Imogen as a student, and realised he could do it quite easily. She would have been exactly as she was now, he thought.

'How did you react?'

'With disbelief at first. Andrew wasn't just my lover, he was my best friend. I couldn't imagine life without him, and it had never occurred to me that he wouldn't feel the same. Then I decided that he was right,' said Imogen. 'It would be best if we had some time apart. So we both went to London, and he got himself a flat and I moved in with Amanda for a while as I was absolutely sure he'd come back. I did a secretarial course, got myself a job and waited for Andrew to miss me.'

'But he didn't?'

'No, he didn't.' Imogen sighed, remembering that time—the slow, sickening realisation that Andrew didn't love her any more. 'I know he's very fond of me, and we've stayed friends, but he didn't need me the way I needed him. I knew in my heart that it was over, but I kept hoping and hoping…'

Her mouth turned down at the memory of her own foolishness. 'And then he met Sara, and it turned out that he needed *her* the way I needed *him*. They got married a couple of years ago, and they're expecting their first baby in the summer.'

Even after all this time it was an effort to keep her voice level.

Tom could see the strain around her eyes and he shifted uncomfortably. He hoped that she wasn't going to cry.

But Imogen was already straightening her shoulders and smiling.

'Do you know the worst thing?' she confided. 'It's that Sara's really *nice*. She makes Andrew happy, and I can see they're perfect for each other. When they got engaged, I used to pray that Andrew would wake up and realise that I was the one he really loved after all, a bit like Julia did with Patrick. I feel awful now to realise I never gave a thought to what that would have been like for Sara.'

Tom shrugged. 'I guess she would have got over it, the way you did. The way I'm going to have to get over it.'

'I hope it doesn't take you as long as it did me,' said Imogen ruefully. 'I've wasted years, convinced that my life was always going to be empty without Andrew. I've tried to meet someone else, but I always end up comparing any man I go out with to him. It took me until last year to really accept that he loves Sara and not me. Even if he stopped loving her for some reason, he still wouldn't love me.

'It's never going to be the way it was before,' she said. 'Andrew moved on a long time ago, and now I need to do that too. I haven't changed since I was a student. It's like I'm stuck in a time warp, where everyone else has moved on and grown up and I've just been drifting, hoping something will change. And, of course, I've realised that the only way something's going to change is if I make it change. If I change myself.'

They had lit the candles on the table, and in the flickering light Tom could see the generous curve of her mouth and the unconsciously upward tilt of her chin. He found himself thinking that it would be a pity if she changed too much.

Imogen sighed a little. 'Anyway, you know what it's like,' she told him. 'I never got as far as planning a wedding, but I understand how it feels when you love someone who decides they don't love you.'

Swirling the dregs of wine in his glass, Tom thought about what she had told him. Imogen always seemed so bright and cheery. He had never guessed that there was a sadness behind her smile.

'I don't feel like that about Julia,' he said abruptly. 'Not the way you felt about Andrew.'

'But you were going to marry her,' said Imogen. 'You must have loved her. You must still love her.'

'Must I?'

Tom's eyes were fixed on the swirling wine, but he was re-membering Julia. 'I desired her, sure, but not with the kind of reckless passion that makes other people lose their heads and, as much as that, I admired her. I still do, I guess. I like her quick wits and cool competence, and I respect everything she's achieved. She worked hard and made a real success of her life. But love her?'

Lifting his eyes to Imogen's face, he shook his head. 'No,' he answered his own question. 'No, I didn't.'

She looked appalled, as if he had kicked away one of the cornerstones of her world, and Tom felt a twinge of remorse, which was ridiculous. 'What?' he said harshly. 'You don't really believe that you have to be in love to get married, do you?'

'But…did Julia know you felt like that?'

'Of course she did. We talked about it when we got engaged, and she said that she felt the same. That's why I was so thrown when she made such a fuss about the wedding.'

Imogen was frowning in bafflement. 'But why get married unless you did love each other? It seems pointless.'

'You don't think it's possible to build a solid marriage based on mutual respect and admiration, and a healthy physical attraction?'

'Maybe, but why would you want to?' she countered. 'I'll only get married if I can find someone who makes me feel the way Andrew did. I want to marry someone I need and who needs me, someone who doesn't think of marriage as a practical arrangement but about being with the one person who fills up all the bits that are missing, who believes that neither of us are complete somehow unless we're together.'

Tom looked uncomprehending, and she tried to explain. 'What's the point of getting married unless you've found the person who makes your heart beat faster, who makes the sun seem brighter, who makes every moment sweeter just by existing? I want to go home at night and be with the one person who can make the rest of the world go away,' she said, 'the one person who, no matter how bad things are, can make it all right just by being there.'

'But that's exactly what I *don't* want,' said Tom, unimpressed. 'I don't want to need anyone else.'

'You don't want to fall in love?'

'No, I don't.' Tom was very definite. 'I've never felt what you felt for Andrew, and I'm glad. You've wasted five years of your life on him, Imogen. Five years! Think of all the things you could have been doing in those five years instead of yearning for the impossible. And knowing what it's like to lose someone you've loved, you're still prepared to risk all that again!'

He shook his head. 'I'd rather have the kind of relationship I had with Julia,' he said. 'True, it ended in humiliation for me, and I can't say I'm happy about it, but my pride is hurt more than my heart. It seems to me that when you fall in love, you lose your senses,' he said. 'You stop thinking clearly. You lose control.'

And that was something Tom Maddison never did.

'Yes, it can make you feel powerless,' Imogen had to admit, remembering how little she had been able to do to make Andrew change his mind. 'You can't make someone love you, that's for sure. But it can also make you feel as if you can do *anything*, and that's always going to be worth the risk.'

'It's not one I'll be taking,' said Tom flatly.

Imogen studied him, mystified. He was a powerful man, much stronger than anyone else she had ever met.

And yet he was afraid of love.

Or was he just afraid of admitting how much he had felt for Julia?

'Well, I'm glad you're OK,' she said at last. 'I thought you must be feeling desperate.'

'I'm fine,' said Tom. 'My ego is massively bruised, but I've got three weeks to recover. I don't think I'll need to take to my bed.'

'Talking of beds…' Imogen hesitated. 'I was thinking I should sleep on one of the couches, and give you the bed.'

'Absolutely not. You're to have the bed.'

'But you're much taller than me,' she protested. 'You'd be much more comfortable in the bed. There are plenty of places I can sleep.'

'I'm not going to be comfortable, knowing that you're stuck on one of those couches, am I?'

'The same goes for me,' she pointed out.

'In that case, the only answer is for us to share the bed.' Tom raised a brow. 'Are you ready to be *that* good friends?'

No, she wasn't, but it was alarming how ready she was to imagine what it would be like, disturbing how easily she could picture sleeping in the big, beautiful bed with Tom beside her. There would be plenty of room for both of them, but nothing to stop her rolling over in the night and finding herself lying against his lean, hard body.

Nothing to stop her snuggling into his back and sliding an arm over him.

And if she did that, what would Tom do? Would he turn over to face her? Would he pull her closer and explore the curves and contours of her body with those strong, sure hands? Would his lips nuzzle her throat before drifting downwards?

Imogen gulped and jammed the brakes on an imagination that was spinning dangerously out of control.

'I think that really *would* be uncomfortable,' she said with a nervous smile.

'Quite.' Tom's voice was very dry and, when the cool grey eyes looked into hers, Imogen was suddenly convinced that he could see right into her mind.

Clumsily, she pushed back her chair, just in case he really had developed an uncanny ability to read her thoughts.

'Well, I think I'll go to bed.' Was that really her voice? Since when had she taken to squeaking?

'It's been a long day,' Tom agreed, getting to his feet as well.

Imogen stood there, not knowing what to do with her hands and not quite sure how to get out of the room. She wouldn't think twice about hugging a friend goodnight.

Tom wasn't an ordinary friend.

But unless she could treat him as one, their conversation tonight would have been a complete waste of time.

Don't be so silly, Imogen scolded herself. They had laughed together. They had talked perfectly easily. Everything had been fine until she'd started thinking about the bed. That had been stupid. The last thing she wanted was to start feeling tense around him again.

So she put on a bright smile and went round the table towards him.

'Goodnight, Tom,' she said, opening her arms.

It was obvious that he wasn't expecting her to hug him. Taken by surprise, he stood rigidly as she pressed her cheek against his, and it was a moment before his arms closed awkwardly around her.

Anyone would think he had never hugged a woman before.

As Imogen stepped back, Tom found his voice at last. 'Goodnight,' he said gruffly.

'Well…' Her smile almost faltered but she pinned it back into place. 'See you in the morning, then.' She turned for the bedroom. 'Sleep well.'

Oh, yes, *sure* he'd sleep well! Easy for Imogen to say, thought Tom as he tried to make himself comfortable on the long sofa. She didn't have to lie in the dark, remembering the feel of her body pressed against him, the feel of her arms around him.

He had been shockingly aware of her softness, of the smoothness of her cheek. The smell of her shampoo and the clean, fresh scent of her skin had struck him like a blow, and when he had recovered enough to respond to her gesture, his hand had rested on the small of her back, and he had felt the soft cotton of her dress shift and slip over her body.

Tom's mouth dried at the memory, and he turned restlessly on the cushions. He should be thinking about Julia. This should have been his wedding night, after all.

He tried to recall the sick churn of rage and humiliation when he had to tell those people Imogen hadn't managed to warn that the wedding was off. He had loathed seeing the sympathy in their eyes, hated knowing that they saw him now as the one who had lost, the one who couldn't make it work, the one they could all feel sorry for. But now, listening to the shrill of the insects in the tropical night and the distant boom of the ocean on the reef, none of it seemed to matter quite so much.

Tom was glad that he hadn't loved Julia the way Imogen had thought he should. If he had, he would be lying here in the dark, longing for her, raging against Patrick, who had strolled in at the last minute and thrown all his careful plans into confusion.

Instead of which, he was remembering how Imogen had looked before she grabbed that towel. He was thinking about Imogen alone in that big bed, and wondering what it would be like to lose himself in that lush, lovely body.

Maybe that wasn't such a good thing.

Imogen… Who would have thought she could look like that? So warm, so soft, so disturbingly, unexpectedly desirable?

Tom punched the cushion beneath his head a few times and tried lying down again. The friends thing had seemed a good idea at the time, but he had a nasty feeling it wasn't going to be that easy in practice.

Especially not if she was going to keep hugging him like that.

Imogen was his PA, for God's sake, he reminded himself savagely. He had barely noticed her before, and now was not the time to start. He didn't want to spend the next three weeks not thinking about her skin, about the curve of her breasts, the silky tumble of her hair, the way her blue eyes reflected the sunshine…

The cushion took another pummelling.

Friends, that was all she had suggested. A friend wouldn't be thinking about that glorious body. A friend wouldn't be fantasising about unzipping that dress, letting it fall in a pool to the floor so that he could explore every inch of that warm, creamy skin.

A friend would remember that she was still more than half in love with her college sweetheart. He would know that she had been hurt and that the last thing she needed was her boss lusting after her body.

No, friends were just…friendly. Friendly was all he could be.

Imogen woke slowly. For a long while she just lay there without thinking, simply savouring the comfort of the bed and the delicious awareness of sunlight striping across her eyelids.

When she opened her eyes at last, the first thing she saw was a huge wooden ceiling fan, turning lazily in the turgid air. At the window, wooden blinds let in bright slivers of light and, as her ears became attuned, she could hear a bird squawking somewhere and the indistinct murmur of the ocean.

In spite of the fan, it was already hot and Imogen stretched luxuriously, filled with a sense of well-being. It wasn't every day you woke up in paradise.

What was she doing in paradise?

Imogen sat bolt upright as she remembered, and she grabbed her watch from the bedside table. It was almost ten o'clock.

Throwing back the sheet, she wrapped a sarong around her and padded into the living area.

It was empty, except for a laptop open on the dining room table, a cursor winking reprovingly at her, but the smell of coffee drew her to the kitchen tucked away behind a room divider, where she found Tom shaking freshly ground beans into a cafetière.

'Good morning,' she said, suddenly shy.

'Morning,' said Tom.

Imogen clearly thought nothing of hugging her friends goodnight, and he was a little nervous in case she greeted them the same way in the morning, so it was a relief to discover that she limited herself to a smile. He had been braced to resist another hug, but he didn't fancy his chances of keeping his hands to himself, especially not when her blue eyes were clouded with sleep, her hair was tousled and she was wrapped only in a strip of cloth that would unwind at the merest brush of his hands.

Tom concentrated fiercely on the coffee. It was all very well resolving to be friendly, but much harder to remember when she stood there, smiling, looking dishevelled and unaccountably desirable.

Friends shouldn't smile like that, he thought crossly. PAs definitely shouldn't. If Imogen hadn't been both, it was the kind of smile that would make him want to take her straight back to bed.

Luckily she *was* his PA, so Tom turned firmly away to pour boiling water into the cafetière.

CHAPTER SIX

'How did you sleep?'

Extraordinarily, his voice sounded almost normal. It would be hard to guess that his throat was tight and his heart was slamming against his ribs.

'Like a log, thank you,' said Imogen. 'What about you? Was the sofa very uncomfortable?'

'It was fine,' said Tom, who had spent a restless night feeling edgy and hot and confused.

'Good. I was feeling guilty about having that comfortable bed.'

She told herself that was what had kept her awake long after Tom had switched off the last light. He had lain out of sight around the corner, but she had still been desperately aware of him.

It was all very well to talk about being normal, but normal would have been to be lying in this bed together, holding each other, touching each other.

Making love.

But they had decided to be friends instead. Friends was much better than being normal.

Wasn't it?

Of course it was.

In the kitchen, there was an awkward pause. 'Want some coffee?' said Tom after a moment.

'Thanks.'

Fastening her sarong more firmly around her, Imogen perched on a stool at the breakfast bar. 'How long have you been up?'

'A couple of hours. I slept late this morning. I'm usually awake about five.'

'That'll be why you're always at the office before me,' said Imogen, who was a night owl and had to be dragged kicking and screaming out of sleep by a piercing alarm every morning in order to get to work on time.

But as soon as the words were out, she wished that she hadn't mentioned the office. It was too bizarre to be sitting here in her sarong, watching Tom make coffee, and remembering that he was her boss and she was just his PA.

Then again, perhaps she *should* remember that more often. Last night, it had been all too easy to forget.

'You've been working,' she said, nodding at the laptop in the other room.

'I thought I might as well see what was going on.' There was a faintly defensive edge to Tom's voice. 'The world hasn't stopped just because we're here. There are still things to do, and I've got to—'

He stopped. 'Why are you looking at me like that?'

'Are you asking me as a PA or as a friend?'

'As a friend,' said Tom after a moment's hesitation.

'OK, then I think you're mad,' she said bluntly. 'You need a break, Tom. If I were you, I'd take that laptop to the end of the jetty and toss it into the lagoon.'

'What?' He looked absolutely horrified at the thought.

'This is supposed to be a holiday. You shouldn't even be *thinking* about work. Why don't you just relax?'

'And do what exactly?'

'You said you would teach me how to snorkel,' she reminded him.

'Hmm.' He *had* said that, Tom remembered, but he wasn't buying the idea of relaxing for three weeks. Who did she think he was? 'What would you have said if I'd asked you as my PA?'

'Certainly, Mr Maddison, what would you like me to do first?'

His mouth twitched. 'I don't remember you ever being that demure in real life!'

'Of course I was,' said Imogen, pretending to bridle. 'I'm the perfect PA.'

'You think so?'

'I'm reliable, aren't I? And discreet. So discreet, in fact, that you hardly knew I was there half the time. What more do you want from a PA?'

'I knew you were there all right,' Tom said. 'You were always talking to someone.'

But he knew what Imogen meant. He hadn't really been aware of her. It was hard to believe now that he had worked with her for six months and never realised that her eyes were that blue, or her skin that soft. How could he not have noticed her body before? He must have been blind.

All that time Imogen had been there, and he hadn't given her more than a passing thought. The office was never going to be the same again, Tom realised with a sinking heart. Now that he *had* noticed her, he wasn't going to be able to stop. He wouldn't be able to walk past her desk without knowing how soft and generously curved she was beneath whatever prim PA outfit she might be wearing.

Without remembering how dishevelled she looked when she had just got out of bed, with her hair all mussed. Without thinking about the way those dark blue eyes danced when she was teasing him, about the feel of her and the scent of her when she hugged him.

Tom rolled a shoulder uneasily. The office had always been the place he felt most comfortable, but it looked as if that was all going to change. Perhaps it was just as well that Imogen would be leaving soon.

'Is there a problem?' Imogen had been watching his face more closely than he realised.

'Problem? No!' he said quickly.

'So are you going to listen to me as a friend or as a secretary?'

'Both,' said Tom, taking a firm grip of himself. 'I'll teach you how to snorkel and we'll go out to the reef, but it'll be very hot by the time we get there so we won't be able to spend too long. When we get back, I want to do some work and I don't want to hear anything about switching off or relaxing or any of that stuff. Deal?'

'Deal!' Imogen jumped off her stool and grinned at him. 'I'll go and get ready.' Her eyes were bright and blue, and she looked so pretty and so vivid that Tom felt his throat close.

He actually had to clear it before he could speak. 'Have you got anything like an old T-shirt with you?' he asked her, forcing his mind back to practicalities. 'You should wear something over your bikini to stop your shoulders getting burnt.'

'Old T-shirts are about all I *have* got,' said Imogen cheerfully. 'I'd have had much more of a problem if you'd asked me to wear something smart.'

It didn't take long to put on a bikini and a T-shirt and she was back a few minutes later, eager to get going.

Tom had been checking the snorkelling equipment and mentally lashing himself. Somehow things had got off track in the last twenty-four hours. He'd come to Coconut Island to save face, to get away from the pitying looks that were bound to follow him once it became known that Julia had jilted him practically at the altar, and to do some work. It had seemed like a good idea at the time.

He just hadn't counted on Imogen being quite so…distracting. It was time to take control, Tom decided. Yes, she was more attractive than he had realised, and yes, the friends thing made sense while they were here but, when it came down to it, she was still his PA. If he wanted to get any work done here, and once they got home, he had better start remembering that. He needed to get things back onto the friendly but impersonal footing he had originally intended.

So it should have helped that Imogen turned up in a baggy old T-shirt unlike anything Julia would ever have worn. He had always been drawn to women who were well-groomed and dressed with style, so the faded T-shirt ought to have been enough on its own to remind him of all the reasons he shouldn't, couldn't, *didn't* find his PA remotely attractive.

Only it didn't work like that. All the T-shirt did was draw his attention to the swell of her breasts, to the curve of her hips and her bare legs. He watched Imogen slathering them with sun cream and found his mouth drying.

Friendly and impersonal? Yeah, right.

Tom forced his eyes back to the flippers he had been sorting through when Imogen had appeared. No staring, no imagining how it would feel to run his hands up and down those legs. No fantasising about peeling that T-shirt off her…

He could do it, Tom told himself sternly. All it took was a little self-control, and control was what he did best.

'Let's go,' he said gruffly as he handed Imogen a snorkel and mask. 'We'll let you practice in the lagoon first, and then we'll go out to the reef.'

He showed her how to put her face in the water and breathe through the snorkel, and when he was satisfied that she had the hang of it, he tossed the flippers and masks into the little dinghy and started the outboard motor.

The morning air sparkled as they puttered out towards reef. From the boat, the house was quickly swallowed by the foliage until the island seemed no more than a low smudge of dark green between the vast blue arch of the sky and the pale jade of the lagoon. Behind them, the engine spluttered water that glinted like diamonds in the sunlight and left a quiet, rippling wake.

Facing him on the hard seat, Imogen's T-shirt was wet from her lesson and it clung in a most distracting way. Tom had been able to ignore it when he was explaining how to breathe through the snorkel, but now it was an effort to keep his eyes on her face instead.

Her hair hung damply to her shoulders, and her skin was bare and already slightly marked from the mask. She was pretty enough, but not stunning, Tom told himself, reassured that he could be so objective.

Barely had he decided that he could relax after all when Imogen lifted her face to the sun with a sigh of pure pleasure, closed her eyes and smiled, and his hand promptly slipped on the helm, making the boat swing round.

Imogen's eyes snapped open at the sudden movement and Tom's muffled curse. 'What's wrong?'

You are, Tom wanted to shout. *You're wrong. You're supposed to just be my PA. Stop smiling like that. Stop looking like that. Stop making me notice you like that.*

'Nothing,' he said curtly instead and pointed at the reef as if he had been planning to end up at that place anyway. 'We'll anchor over there.'

When the boat was secured, he handed Imogen her flippers and waited until her mask and snorkel were in place before he helped her over the side and into the water. He couldn't do it without touching her, and he was very aware of her arm beneath his hand as he steadied her.

Imogen hung on to the edge of the boat, getting used to the feel of the mask clamped tightly to her face and the snorkel that filled her mouth awkwardly. She watched Tom put on his own flippers and drop neatly into the water beside her, and couldn't help contrasting it with her own lumbering efforts.

Tom surfaced, pulling the snorkel from his mouth and pushing the mask up onto his forehead. 'OK?'

He was very close. Through her mask, Imogen could see him in startling, stomach-clenching detail. His pale eyes were extraordinarily clear in the bright light, contrasting with the darkness of his lashes and the heavy brows. His hair was wet, and droplets of water clung to his face.

She stared at them, half mesmerised by the way they accentuated the texture of his skin, the lines creasing beside his eyes, the roughness of his jaw, and as a drop trickled down towards that firm, cool mouth, Imogen felt as if a hard fist had closed around her lungs and was methodically squeezing out all the air.

Confused by the snorkel, she pulled it out of her mouth so that she could draw a fresh lungful of air and felt immediately better.

'OK,' she confirmed, using her flippers to move away from him in what she hoped was a casual gesture.

He was too close, too overwhelming. It seemed impossible that this was Tom Maddison, that only four days ago they had been in the London office, and he had just been her boss.

He was still just her boss, Imogen reminded herself firmly.

'OK,' she said again.

'Stay close,' said Tom, pulling down his mask. 'And don't touch anything. Just look.'

Imogen nodded, took a breath and replaced the snorkel.

She had a momentary panic when she put her face into the water, but then she remembered to breathe as Tom had taught her and the next moment she was floating in the water and looking down at a different world.

Entranced, she drifted along the reef, needing only the occasional gentle movement of the flippers to propel her through the water. It was cooler here, and a lovely deep, dark blue that somehow managed to be clear at the same time so that through the mask she could look right down to the bottom of the lagoon far below. If these were the shallows, how deep was the ocean on the other side of the reef?

Imogen had never seen so many fish before or such vividly coloured creatures. She was a city girl, and in her limited experience British wildlife tended to be brown and grey and black, colours that blended into a drab winter landscape. In comparison, the reef was startlingly bright, with a palatte to rival that of the most colourful of fashion designers. The fish swimming beneath her were coloured in blues, greens, yellows, reds and every shade in between, as if a child had been let loose with a box of crayons. They were extraordinarily patterned too, with bold stripes and pretty speckles and strange splodges in a spectacularly gaudy combination of colours.

She had always imagined that coral would be white and bony, but it, too, came in a bizarre range of colours and shapes as it dropped away into the depths. The sun bounced on the surface of the water, filtering down until it caught shoals of tiny fish, invisible until they flashed in the light. Tom touched her arm and pointed down and Imogen's eyes widened at the sight of a huge green fish with a ponderous pout that seemed to be lumbering around the coral outcrops in comparison with the smaller fish that flickered around it.

Imogen was enthralled, but acutely aware at the same time of the sound of her breathing, abnormally loud and eerily laboured through the snorkel, of the feel of the T-shirt wafting around her as she drifted, and of Tom's reassuring presence beside her.

Every now and then a fish would swim up to stare dispassionately into her mask but for the most part they seemed oblivious of the humans hanging in the water above them. There were fish everywhere, swimming along the reef with stately grace, some moving languorously amongst the coral, others darting, drifting, nibbling at tiny plants, flicking busily to and fro. Whole shoals moved as if they were one, accelerating at some unseen signal, and turning together in a shimmer of light.

Absorbed in the magic world beneath her, Imogen was disappointed when Tom touched her arm again and pointed back to the boat but, remembering the deal they had made, she followed him reluctantly.

'That was *fantastic*!' she said as she threw the mask into the boat and clambered awkwardly in after it, too excited by what she had seen to care what she looked like. 'The fish are amazing. I can't *believe* the colours.'

She talked on, squeezing the worst of the wetness from her T-shirt and tipping her head from one side to the other to shake the water out of her ears.

There was a big red mark on her face where the rubber mask had been clamped to her skin, but her eyes were shining and her expression so vivid with delight that Tom felt his throat tighten.

'We can come out again tomorrow if you like, but you've had enough for today,' he said gruffly. 'You'd get burnt if you stayed out much longer.'

'I think you might be right,' said Imogen reluctantly, twisting her legs round as far as she could. 'I can already feel the backs of my thighs tingling.'

Tom couldn't afford to let himself think about her thighs,

or about the way that wet T-shirt clung to her body again. He started the motor with an unnecessarily vigorous jerk of the cord and for the umpteenth time reminded himself what he was doing there.

'We've got work to do, too,' he told Imogen, who was clearly having trouble mustering any enthusiasm at the prospect, although she nodded readily enough.

'Of course,' she said in her best PA voice.

Ali had been in while they were out, and the house was beautifully clean and tidy. The fridge was full of wonderful things to eat, and the bed made with crisp, fresh sheets. Imogen wondered if Ali had noticed that the bed was strangely unrumpled for a honeymoon suite.

'It's like living in a magic castle where jobs get done before you think of them,' she said, helping herself to some fruit. 'I wish I could take Ali home with me.'

'I don't suppose he's checked the stock markets or caught up on all those reports yet,' said Tom caustically. 'There are still some jobs we'll have to do ourselves.'

'Oh, yes.' Reminded of what she was supposed to be doing, Imogen licked pineapple juice off her fingers. 'Is it OK if I have a quick shower first?'

'Good idea,' said Tom, who didn't fancy his chances of concentrating on work if she was sitting there in that wet T-shirt.

It was time to be professional, he decided, opening his laptop a little while later, after he had had a shower of his own. In spite of the heat, he wished he could put on his suit and tie, instead of shorts and a short-sleeved shirt, which was the best he could do for now. He wished he were back in his office in London, in fact, where he was never distracted and where Imogen only ever wore…well, he didn't know what she wore, but that was the whole point. He never noticed her there at all.

As it was, Imogen had appeared in loose trousers and a

sleeveless top. She had done her best to find something appropriate to wear, Tom supposed grudgingly. It wasn't her fault that her hair was still wet, or that her top only seemed to emphasise the shadow of her cleavage. Or that he couldn't stop remembering the sheer delight in her face, the smoothness of her skin when he'd steadied her in the boat.

It wasn't her fault that, for the first time in his life, he didn't know exactly what he wanted, and being unable to focus on a goal left him feeling restless and faintly uneasy.

They did try. They sat across from each other at the table and began by checking their email, but it was hard to care very much about strategic audits or core competencies or competitor analysis when outside the ocean was murmuring against the reef and the sun was slicing through the fringed leaves of the coconuts. Somewhere a bird called raucously and a tiny, almost colourless gecko ran up the wall and froze as if astounded by the sight of two humans staring silently at their computer screens.

Tom couldn't understand it. Until now, work had always been his refuge. He was famous for his ability to focus, in fact, but the words on his computer screen were dancing before his eyes, and his attention kept straying to Imogen across the table. Had she always had that little crease between her brows when she studied the screen? That way of tucking her hair behind her ears?

Sensing his gaze, she glanced up and caught him staring at her. 'Did you want something?' she asked.

Tom scowled to cover his mortification. 'We ought to discuss the new acquisitions strategy.'

'O-kay,' said Imogen cautiously while she racked her brain to remember what he was talking about. Her mind was full of colourful fish and the sunlight on the sea. She couldn't even remember what an acquisition was, let alone how you ever had a strategy for it. London and the office seemed to belong to a different world altogether, a world where Tom Maddison was brusque and brisk and besuited, not lean and long-legged and sleekly muscled.

Not the kind of man who could make her heart turn over just by sitting at the helm of a boat with his hair lifting in the breeze from the ocean and his steely eyes turned to silver in the light.

Tom started talking about some new executive vice president while Imogen searched her inbox desperately for the relevant email, until he stopped abruptly.

'Oh, to hell with it!' he said, throwing up his hands in a gesture of defeat. 'It's too hot to work. Let's go and swim.'

'I've often wondered how people who live in lovely climates ever get any work done,' said Imogen a little while later. They were sitting in the tattered shade of a leaning palm and she curled her toes in the soft sand as she looked out over the lagoon. 'It's bad enough at home when the sun shines. The moment it comes out, I always feel like turning off my computer and spending the afternoon in the park.'

Tom raised a brow. 'Nice to know you've got such dedication to your work.'

'I'm only a temp,' Imogen reminded him, unruffled by his sarcasm. 'Temps aren't supposed to be dedicated. It's different for you. You're responsible for the whole company. If you get it wrong—or decide you'd rather spend the afternoon in the park—then it's not just you that's out of a job. A lot of other people will lose their jobs too.' She made a face. 'I'd hate to have that kind of pressure on me, which is why I'll never have a hugely successful career.'

'Don't you have any ambition?' said Tom, unable to completely conceal his disapproval.

'Sure I do, but it's probably not the kind you would recognise. My ambition is to be happy,' she said simply. Picking up a piece of the dried coconut husk that littered the sand beneath the trees, she twirled it absently between her fingers. 'To see the world, forget about Andrew and find someone who will love me and who wants to build a life with me.'

Imogen glanced at Tom. She could tell that he didn't understand. 'What about you?' she said, pointing the piece of husk at him as if it were a microphone. 'What's your ambition?'

He didn't have to think about it. 'To be the best.'

'Yes, but the best at what?'

Tom shrugged. He would have thought it was obvious. 'At whatever I'm doing,' he said with a hint of impatience. 'If I'm running a company, I'm going to make it the leader in its field, I'm going to win the most lucrative contracts and earn the highest profits. It doesn't matter what the race is for, I'm going to win it.'

'What happens when you *don't* win?'

'I try again until I do,' said Tom. 'The winner is always the one in control, and I never want to be in a position where anyone else can tell me what to do.'

Imogen tossed the husk back into the sand. 'No wonder you don't believe in love,' she said, remembering their conversation the night before.

'I believe in success,' he said. 'And it's not just for me. I take a failing company, I turn it round and I make it the best and, as you pointed out, everyone who works there shares in that success. People are depending on me for their jobs, for their futures. If I fail, they fail too.'

'They'll still have jobs if the company has the second-highest profits,' Imogen pointed out. 'Not winning isn't always the same as failing.'

'It is to me. I'm not prepared to be second-best,' he said uncompromisingly. 'That's why I won't take a day off when the sun shines.'

'And why you're thinking about work when you're sitting in paradise?' She gestured at the view. Coconut palms bent out towards the water, framing the beach and the lagoon between their fringed leaves like an exquisite picture. Beyond the shade the light was hot and harsh, bouncing off the surface of the lagoon and turning the white sand into a glare.

Tom's expression relaxed a little. 'You started it,' he said.

'Did I?'

'You were the one talking about switching off your computer.'

'So I was,' she conceded. She watched a breath of wind shiver across the surface of the lagoon and stir the palms above their head.

'It's hard to imagine that the office exists right now, isn't it?' she went on after a while. 'While we're sitting here in the sun, the girls are in Reception, Neville's in Finance, the other secretaries are sending out for coffee… There are meetings going on and decisions being taken and things are changing without us.' She shook her head. 'It just doesn't seem real.'

'And when we go back, this won't seem real,' warned Tom.

'Well, I for one am going to make the most of it.' Getting up, Imogen dragged her lounger out of the shade. 'I think I'll spend a busy afternoon working on my tan.'

She adjusted the lounger so that she could lie flat and turned onto her stomach before groping around in the sand for the book she had dropped there. Wriggling into a more comfortable position, she smoothed out the page with a sigh of pleasure.

'This is the life! I'm never going to be able to go back to work after three weeks of this.'

Tom watched her with a mixture of disapproval and envy. She had an extraordinary ability to enjoy the moment, he realised. It wasn't something that he had ever been able to do. He was always too busy thinking about what needed to be done at work.

'Careful you don't get burnt.'

'Yes, Mum!' But Imogen pulled the beach bag towards her and rummaged for the sun cream. She supposed she should put some on. Sunstroke was no fun.

Squeezing some lotion into her palm, she slapped it onto her shoulders as best she could.

Tom hesitated, torn between the disquieting temptation of touching her the way he had been thinking about all day and a horrible fear that he might not be able to control himself if he did.

But she couldn't reach her back herself, could she? He could hardly sit here and let her burn.

'Would you like me to put some cream on your back for you?' he offered stiltedly.

It was Imogen's turn to hesitate. The thing was, she would and she wouldn't. The thought of his hands on her skin made her shiver with excitement, but she was petrified in case he guessed quite how much she *would* like it.

But they were being normal here, right? She would burn if she didn't do something about her back, and she wouldn't hesitate to ask any other friend to rub cream in for her.

'That would be great,' she said after a beat.

Reaching behind her, she unclipped the bikini top and lay flat, her arms folded beneath her face and her head pillowed on her hands. She was wearing sunglasses, but turned her head away from him as an extra precaution.

The squirt of the suntan lotion onto his hands seemed unnaturally loud, and Imogen found herself tensing in preparation for his touch. When it came, his hands were so warm and so sure that she sucked in an involuntary breath and couldn't prevent a small shiver snaking down her spine.

'Sorry, is it cold?'

'No, it's fine.' Imogen's voice was muffled in her hands.

Crouching beside her, Tom smoothed cream firmly over her shoulders and up to the nape of her neck, before his hands, slippery with oil, slid down her back, then up, then down again, spreading his fingers this time to make sure her sides were covered.

Imogen made herself lie still but inside she was squirming with such pleasure that she was afraid that she would actually dissolve, leaving a sticky puddle on the lounger. At the same time she was rigid with tension caused by the need not to show it. She mustn't sigh with pleasure, mustn't roll over, mustn't beg him not to stop…

Oh, God, he had started on the backs of her legs now… Imogen squeezed her eyes shut. Thank goodness she had had them waxed before she'd left.

Tom's hands swept down her thighs in firm strokes to the backs of her knees, then on down to her ankles, before gliding all the way back up again. In spite of her best efforts, Imogen quivered.

She was sure that he must be able to hear her entire body thumping and thudding in time with her pounding heart. Part of her was desperate for him to stop before she disgraced herself by spontaneously combusting, but when he did take his hands away abruptly she only stopped herself from groaning with disappointment in the nick of time.

'That should do you.'

If Imogen had been able to hear anything above the boom of her own pulse she might have noticed the undercurrent of strain to his voice but, as it was, all she could do was lie there and hope that he couldn't actually see the heat beating along her veins.

'Thank you.' Her mouth was so dry, it came out as barely more than a croak.

Tom stood up. 'I think I'll get back to work,' he said curtly. 'No, you stay there,' he added as Imogen lifted her head to ask if he wanted her to do anything. 'There's no point in wasting that lotion. I've just got a few things I want to be getting on with.'

'Well, if you're sure…'

'I'm sure,' said Tom. He badly needed to be alone, and the last thing he wanted was Imogen there, wondering why he was so tense or walking so stiffly! 'I'll see you later.'

There *were* things he needed to do but, no matter how hard he stared at the computer screen, Tom didn't seem to be able to focus. His fingers were still throbbing with the feel of her body, so soft and smooth and warm, so dangerously enticing beneath his hands. Even though he had been able to see that she was rigid with discomfort, he had itched to turn her over, to brush the skimpy bikini away and explore every dip and curve of her.

It had taken every ounce of self-control he possessed to take his hands off her and step back.

Tom rubbed a hand over his face in exasperation at himself. Control, that was the key word here.

Control was what he was best at. It was what he *was*. He had never had any trouble controlling impulses before and there was no reason to start now. It was just the heat and the light getting to him, Tom told himself. Or maybe just a reaction to Julia's rejection. That would be understandable enough.

He began to feel a bit better. Yes, all he needed was a little time on his own out of the sun. He would sit here and work, and he wouldn't think about Imogen at all.

He would be fine.

CHAPTER SEVEN

TOM was still at his computer a couple of hours later when Imogen climbed the steps to the veranda. He looked up as she appeared in the doorway and, as their eyes met, the air quivered on the verge of tension before they both looked away.

'Bored?' he asked.

Imogen laughed and shook her head. 'Hardly! I'm thirsty, though, so I came up to get a drink.' She opened the fridge door to find the water. 'How are you getting on? Is everything under control?'

'It is,' said Tom with satisfaction. There was his word again: *control*. It felt right.

He was feeling much more himself. He had read a couple of reports, and fired off some emails. Under normal circumstances, that would have been the work of half an hour, but it wasn't bad, given the amount of time he had spent carefully not thinking about Imogen.

Imogen poured herself a long glass of water and leant against the room divider to drink it.

'I was thinking I might try walking around the island,' she said tentatively.

Left alone, she had found it impossible to concentrate on her book. She was horribly afraid that Tom might have guessed the effect that he was having on her and had been embarrassed. He hadn't been able to wait to get away!

Not that she blamed him. If she had been rubbing lotion onto someone who squirmed like that, she'd have run a mile too.

He had only been putting a bit of cream on her, for heaven's sake! It had been ridiculous to get herself in a state about it, thought Imogen, mortified. They were supposed to be friends, and friends didn't go to pieces the moment the other laid a finger on them. She was determined to find some way to show him that she was back to normal.

'Are you still working, or would you like to come?'

Tom linked his arms above his head and stretched. 'A walk sounds good.' It sounded normal, easy, safe. Controllable. 'I could do with stretching my legs.'

'Great.' Imogen finished her water. 'I'll get my hat.'

It was well into the afternoon by the time they set out, but it was still very hot, in spite of a breeze that ruffled the lagoon and made the palms sigh and rustle overhead as Imogen and Tom headed barefoot along the beach. Imogen had wrapped a sarong around her waist and her face was shaded by a soft straw hat. Beside her, Tom wore shorts and a loose short-sleeved shirt.

They walked in silence at first but, rather to Imogen's surprise, it didn't feel uncomfortable. They splashed around the point where the dense vegetation grew right to the shore and found themselves on the far side of the island. There was little sand to speak of there, but the water was so warm and clear that they were happy to wade ankle deep in the shallows to where the shore curved inwards once more.

Suddenly Tom stopped and shaded his eyes as he looked out to sea. 'Look!'

'What is it?' Imogen's gaze followed his finger until she exclaimed in delight. 'Dolphins!'

In silence they stood and watched a whole pod of dolphins

leaping out of the water with breathtaking grace. For Imogen, it was an extraordinary moment. It was as if she had never been fully alive before that moment, and she was aware of everything with a new and fierce intensity.

The sea was the bluest of blues, the heat hammered down, the light beyond the shade of her hat glared. She could feel the sand cool beneath her toes, the shallows rippling warm against her ankles and Tom, still and self-contained beside her, while further out the dolphins played, soaring into the air as if for the sheer joy of it, the water that streamed from their bodies glittering in the fierce sunlight.

Imogen could feel her heart swelling and her throat closed at the rush of emotion. The beauty and exuberance of the scene was so joyous it felt like an unexpected gift.

'Quite something, isn't it?' said Tom.

Unable to speak, she nodded.

After a while the dolphins moved on. Imogen and Tom waited a few minutes in case they came back, but eventually they started walking again.

'I'm sorry Julia's not here with you,' she said quietly at last, 'but I'm glad I came. I'll never forget that, or the reef this morning.'

Tom glanced down but could see little of her expression beneath her hat. 'I'm glad you came too,' he said.

Imogen took a breath. 'How are you feeling?' she asked. 'I mean, really?'

'About Julia? I'm OK,' he said when she nodded. 'And yes, *really*.' He looked away from her, squinting slightly at the bright light bouncing off the water. 'Maybe I should be thinking about her more,' he said slowly. 'I wanted to marry her, after all. I ought to be missing her, but the truth is that I'm not. We never actually lived together, so perhaps it's because I'm not used to her being around.'

He fell silent, thinking about the woman who should have been exploring the island with him. What would it have been like to have been here with Julia? Somehow it was hard to imagine when Imogen was walking beside him, her face shaded by the wide brim of her hat. Her skin was glowing after a day in the sun and he could see the salt drying on her shoulders.

The bottom of her sarong was wet and kept clinging to her calves so that every few yards she had to stop and disentangle herself. As she bent, her tangled brown hair would swing forwards and cover her face until she pushed it impatiently behind her ear.

'I think I miss the idea of Julia more than anything else,' Tom went on at last. 'She was so exactly the kind of woman I'd always imagined marrying: beautiful, very intelligent, glamorous, successful…'

All things she wasn't, Imogen couldn't help thinking.

'Well, you've met her,' he said, unaware of her mental interruption. 'You know how special she was. I was tired of girlfriends constantly demanding attention, insisting that I rang them all the time, forever wanting to cross-examine me about my feelings…'

Tom shuddered at the memory. 'They all seemed to think that I could drop everything at work to dance attendance on them and take them out to dinner or to Paris for the weekend, and if there was a crisis at work, they would sulk.' He lifted a shoulder, irritable at the mere memory. 'I couldn't be bothered with any of that.

'Julia was different,' he remembered after a moment. 'She wasn't needy or emotional, and she didn't expect me to jump through hoops for her. We understood each other—or, at least, I thought we did,' he amended. 'I had no idea what Patrick meant to her, for instance. When she said that he was just a friend, I never questioned it. I thought she would be the perfect wife.'

He paused, remembering. 'I suppose the truth is that it wasn't her I really wanted, but someone to go home to. Someone who would make me comfortable, who would be able to cope with any corporate entertaining and who wouldn't make a fuss about the time I spent at work.'

'It sounds to me as if you wanted a housekeeper, not a wife,' said Imogen with a certain tartness. 'Why didn't you just hire someone?'

'Because I don't sleep with my employees.' Tom's voice was level, and Imogen flushed beneath her hat.

Of course he would expect to sleep with his wife, but she didn't really need to have that fact rammed down her throat. She didn't need to imagine being that wife, making love with him every night, waking up with him every morning. Especially when it was never going to happen.

'As one of your employees, that's good to know,' she said as crisply as she could.

Tom slanted her a quick look. 'It's not just about sex,' he said. 'I wanted an equal, someone I could talk to, someone to support me—what was so wrong with that?'

'That depends on what you were going to offer her in return.'

'A lot of money,' he said. 'Security. Comfort. Trust. Respect. Honesty. Fidelity. When I make a promise, I keep it. I wouldn't have taken wedding vows unless I was going to stick to them.'

It wasn't a bad deal, Imogen supposed. She knew people who had settled for less.

He had offered Julia everything except love. Imogen wasn't surprised that Julia had thought that she would marry him, but it wasn't a surprise either that she hadn't been able to go through with it.

Tom might not think love mattered, but it did.

'You don't approve?' He was watching her more closely than she realised.

'It's not up to me to approve or disapprove,' said Imogen carefully. 'It just wouldn't be enough for me.'

'What more do you want? Oh—love, I suppose?'

'Yes, love,' she said evenly, ignoring the dismissive note in his voice. 'What good is respect or security or all that stuff if you're not with someone who makes you feel…oh, I don't know…'

How could she explain to someone like Tom? '…like one of those dolphins we saw,' she tried. 'They looked so…so *joyous* leaping out of the water, didn't they? As if they were exactly where they wanted to be, doing exactly what they wanted to do. That's how it feels when you're in love,' she told him. 'I'm not getting married until I feel that way again.'

Tom shook his head, unconvinced. 'You're not being realistic, Imogen. You want everything to be perfect, but nothing ever is. Look at Coconut Island,' he said, gesturing around him. 'They said it was paradise, and it is—but there are still cockroaches and bats and who knows what else lurking in the undergrowth.'

Imogen cast a nervous glance at the vegetation smothering the shore. She hadn't thought about what else might be sharing the island with them and wished that Tom hadn't put the idea into her head. What if there were snakes? Mentally resolving to stick to the beach at all times, she edged further out into the water.

Tom was still talking about the need to adjust her ideas. 'You're holding on to a fantasy,' he told her.

'So I've been told,' said Imogen with a slight edge. 'Amanda thinks I ought to compromise, and go out with men who aren't absolutely perfect, but I don't want to do that. I've been in love. OK, it didn't work out, but I'm not prepared to settle for anything less.'

'You're just setting yourself up for disappointment,' he warned, and she put up her chin.

'Well, we'll have to agree to disagree, won't we? It's just as well we're not thinking of getting married, isn't it?'

There was a tiny pause. In spite of himself, Tom's mind flickered to Imogen's warm, smooth body, to the feel of her hug and the laughter in her eyes. It might be nice to go home to that every night.

But that would mean feeling unsettled the whole time. Imogen would want him to love her and make her feel like a bloody dolphin! Tom recoiled from the very thought. His whole life would slip out of control in no time. No, he couldn't cope with that at all.

'Yes,' he agreed. 'Just as well.'

That first day set the pattern for the week. Walking round the island at the end of the afternoon became part of their routine. Imogen never got tired of the reef and was eager to get out there every morning. For the first couple of days, she sat down at her computer when they got back, but in the end Tom told her gruffly that there was little point in her being there and that she could do as she pleased.

Imogen didn't put up much of a protest, it had to be said. It was impossible to concentrate, anyway, and she hoped that eventually Tom would get the idea of not working as well and learn to relax instead.

Not that there was much sign of that yet. Imogen had no idea what he was doing, but he seemed to spend hours at his laptop while she was on the beach. It was a shame that he was such a workaholic, she thought. He wasn't having much of a holiday and, when they did spend time together, they were getting on surprisingly well. Sometimes he would bring her a drink, or join her for a swim, but he never stayed for long and always made an excuse to get back to his computer.

Tom was not, in fact, doing nearly as much work as Imogen

thought he was. Oh, he spent a lot of time sitting and looking at the screen but he was finding it increasingly hard to concentrate.

Imogen was a constant distraction, and his mind had a disturbing tendency to drift towards her at inappropriate times and in frankly inappropriate ways. It made Tom very uneasy. He had never had this problem focusing before.

The truth was that he was deeply tempted to succumb to this unexpected attraction, but how could it possibly work? When it came down it, Imogen was still his PA and it was hardly any time since he was supposed to be marrying Julia. She wasn't going to believe him if he told her that he was fast becoming obsessed with her, was she?

Of course, it was just a physical obsession, Tom reassured himself, and obviously well under his control. Which was just as well, given that Imogen was clinging to her ridiculous fantasy about love.

No, it would never work. Besides, none of this would seem real when he got home, Tom would remind himself whenever he wavered from his decision. It was all too easy to get carried away by the seductive glitter of sunlight on the lagoon and the hot, starry nights. Back in his cool, well-ordered London life he would be very glad that he hadn't made a move.

In the meantime, he was doing his best to maintain some distance. It was a little easier once he had told Imogen that he didn't expect her to work after all. Tom had been afraid that if she carried on sitting across the table from him she would realise just how little work he was actually doing.

Otherwise, things were OK if they were doing something—snorkelling or swimming or walking or eating—but he avoided the beach as much as possible. When Imogen was just *there*, looking touchable, his hands would start to twitch alarmingly and he had to take himself off in case they reached for her of their own accord.

The evenings were tricky too, but at least then it was dark. Together, they would sit and watch, mesmerised, while the sky softened and glowed and the sun sank towards the horizon and disappeared at last in an extravaganza of fiery colour. The sudden darkness brought a raucous chorus of insects and the bats, swooping and diving through the hot air.

Tom was always achingly aware of Imogen beside him then. Every evening she showered and changed into a dress, and he could smell the soap and sunshine on her skin, and in the freshly washed hair that tumbled loose to her shoulders.

But he could handle it. It was under control.

'I don't like the look of that.' Imogen stopped in the shallows and pointed at the horizon, which was boiling with dark, dense, billowy clouds.

It was very hot and even the water around her ankles felt warmer than usual. The circuit of the island involved more wading than walking, but it was already familiar. Imogen did a quick calculation. This was the fifth time they had done it, but the first time she had noticed clouds like that. They were a long way away, it was true, but there was something menacing about them, and she watched them uneasily.

'I hope there's not going to be a storm.'

Tom eyed the horizon. 'It's looking pretty black,' he agreed. 'We might well get some rain.'

'I don't mind rain. It's thunder and lightning that make me nervous.' Imogen hugged her arms together. 'I know it's silly, but I hate storms.

'When I was little, I went on a camping trip with my friend and her family,' she said. 'We were staying on a campsite by a river, and there was a terrific storm in the middle of the night. Thunder, lightning, torrential rain, wind…the full works. It was chaos,' she remembered with a

shudder. 'There were tents blowing away, and people screaming and the river flooded…

'I was only seven and I was terrified, although it turned out
in the end that no one had been badly hurt or anything. But
the tents were ruined and everything was such a mess that we
went back early. When we got home, my mother had to tell
me that my granny had died suddenly while I'd been away.'

The memory still made Imogen sad. 'She'd been living
with us and I absolutely adored her. I was devastated, and I
suppose it got all muddled up in my mind. I thought that the
storm had somehow killed Granny, and the next time there
was thunder and lightning I got absolutely hysterical.'

Tom's expression was hard to read and she trailed off,
feeling foolish. 'I told you it was silly,' she apologised.

'It's difficult to get things that happen to us as kids into
proper perspective,' he said. 'Even when we're grown up and
understand what really happened, we still feel it the way we
did then. My mother died when I was five,' he said abruptly.
'I don't remember much about her—it's more of an impression than a specific memory—but I remember exactly the
tweedy jacket my father was wearing when he came back
from hospital to tell me. It felt rough when he hugged me, and
I can still see those leather buttons. Even now I'll sometimes
catch a glimpse of someone wearing a jacket like that and I'll
feel a mixture of confusion and distress, just like I did then.'

He had kept his account deliberately dispassionate, but
Imogen felt tears sting her eyes at the thought of the small boy
learning that his world had fallen apart.

'How awful for you.'

'I was all right.' She was unsurprised when Tom brushed her
sympathy aside and carried on splashing through the shallows.

'I don't think I really understood what my father meant,'
he said. 'They hadn't told me that she was ill, and I was just

aware that nothing was happening as it should any more. I remember not understanding why the house was a mess or why we didn't have meals at the proper times any more.

'Of course, I can see now that my father was struggling to cope, and doing the best that he could. Tidying the house wouldn't have been top of his order of priorities, but it bothered me at the time. That level of disorder still makes me uncomfortable,' he added in a burst of confidence.

No wonder being in control was so important to him, thought Imogen, wading through the warm water beside him. His mother's death would have disrupted everything that he took for granted. As a small boy, he must have felt utterly powerless. She could see how building an orderly world that he could control would be a way of coping with the loss of the most important figure in his life.

His distrust of emotions made more sense now. Tom might think that he was being realistic, but inside he was still the boy who had lost the woman he loved the most, and was afraid of feeling that bereft again. It was easy to see how a small child, unable to understand death, would think that he had been abandoned by his mother, would feel at some level that she wouldn't have left him if he'd been good enough. That would certainly explain his drive to succeed, to prove again and again that he *was* good enough.

And now Julia had abandoned him too. Imogen's heart cracked for him, and she slid a glance under her lashes. She knew better than to say anything, but she felt desperately sorry for him. It wasn't surprising that he was so wary of love. Falling in love would mean letting go of everything that had made him feel safe since he was a child.

It was a shame, Imogen thought. If only Tom would take the risk, he could make some woman very happy. Behind that brusque exterior was a man who was strong and steady and fiercely intelligent, with an unexpectedly dry sense of humour. The more time she spent with him, the more she found herself liking him.

And the more attractive she found him.

Night after night, she would lie alone in the big bed and think about Tom on the sofa, just round the corner. In the darkness she would remember how he looked when he came out of the water, brushing his wet hair back from his forehead. His legs were long and lean, his chest broad and his shoulders powerful. Imogen's mouth would dry at the memory.

It was getting harder and harder to remember that she was supposed to be treating him like any other friend. She was reluctant to offer to rub sun cream into his back too often, not because she didn't want to touch him, but because she wanted it too much. Tom often hesitated before accepting, and Imogen was convinced that he knew how much she loved the sensation of feeling the leashed power of his body beneath her hands, in spite of her best attempts to appear brisk and unconcerned. His skin was warm and sleek and matt and, when she felt his muscles flex at her touch, her stomach tightened and heat roiled through her.

It was all she could do to stop her hands sliding all over him. She longed to explore all that solidity and strength, to touch her lips to the back of his neck and kiss her way down his spine and then turn him over and start all over again. Sometimes Imogen felt quite giddy with it, and snapping the lid back on the bottle and stepping back took such a heroic effort that she had to sit down and close her eyes.

And remind herself of all the reasons why she had to keep her hands firmly to herself.

It would be a huge mistake to forget how incompatible they were. She might understand now why Tom was so resistant to the idea of love, but that didn't change the facts. She would be mad to even think about falling for a man who was incapable of loving her back. All he could ever offer was a physical relationship, and that wouldn't be enough for her.

Would it?

'It's hot tonight.'

Dropping onto the wicker seat next to Tom's, Imogen lifted the hair from her neck in a vain attempt to cool it and he got a whiff of shampoo. He couldn't recognise the scent—limes, perhaps, and something else—but it was clean and fresh and innocently alluring, rather, he realised with something approaching dismay, like Imogen herself.

She was wearing loose silky trousers tonight, but with a strappy top that left her arms and shoulders bare. Tom was sure that she hadn't set out to look seductive, but all she had to do was sit there in her very ordinary clothes and he was wondering what it would be like to run his hands down those smooth arms, wondering how warm her skin would feel, how easily those tiny strips would slide from her shoulders…

Swallowing, he got up to make her a drink. 'I think we may be getting that rain soon,' he said. When in doubt, stick to the weather.

'Really?' Imogen looked out at the lagoon with a frown. In the last flush of the sunset, it gleamed like burnished copper, its surface glassy and still.

'It's very close,' he pointed out, 'and those clouds were behind us, remember? Just because we can't see them doesn't mean they're not there.'

Imogen pulled a face. 'Creepy thought.' Not being able to see it only made the gathering storm seem more menacing.

Uneasily, she pulled her legs up so that she could hug her knees. 'I think you must be right, though. It feels eerie tonight. It's as if the whole island is holding its breath.'

The air was suffocatingly hot and heavy. It seemed to wrap itself around them as Tom handed Imogen her drink and sat back down beside her.

'Listen!' he said, holding up a finger.

Imogen cocked her head on one side. 'I can't hear anything.'

'Exactly. Usually you can't hear yourself think for the insects but there's not a peep out of them tonight. It's all quiet.'

'So it is.' In spite of the heat, she shivered. 'No bats either. It's uncanny.'

The last stripe of scarlet along the horizon slipped away and the darkness swooped after it, swallowing up the last gleam of light in the sky. It felt more intense than usual, and Imogen was sure that she could feel the blackness boiling angrily up behind them.

The silence was making her stomach churn, and she bit her lip and hugged her knees more tightly, unsure whether she longed for something to happen to break the suspense, or dreaded it.

A lamp inside threw a dim yellow glow through the window onto the veranda. It was enough for Tom to see a pulse hammering in Imogen's throat. Her whole body was rigid with tension, and he remembered what she had told him earlier about her fear of storms.

'Come here,' he said, and held out his hand.

Imogen didn't even hesitate. She took it gratefully, and the fear that had been jittering just below her skin steadied the moment his fingers closed firmly around hers. His clasp was warm and strong as he drew her down onto the seat close beside him. He didn't tell her not to be frightened, but just put his arm around her and held her close against the hard security of his body.

Her heart was booming and thudding, but now she didn't know whether it was from fear or from a desperate, churning awareness of Tom's nearness. He was so solid, so steady, so gloriously reassuring, that she wanted to burrow into him, but she made herself sit still, comforted by the strength of his arm.

As every evening, he was wearing cool chinos and a loose shirt. Tonight, for the first time, she was close enough to feel that it was made of the finest cotton, close enough to breathe in its indefinably expensive smell, mingled with the clean, wonderfully male scent of his skin.

Imogen was so distracted by the feel of him that she almost forgot the threatening storm until the blackness was fractured by a great fork of lightning, followed a few seconds later by an ear-splitting crack that sent her heart lurching into her throat.

Tom felt her jump and tightened his arm around her. 'Here we go,' he said cheerfully. 'Looks like it's going to be a big one, but you're safe with me.'

And, incredibly, safe was exactly how Imogen felt, even though the sky was lit up again and again in a spectacular display, and the sound of the thunder ripped through the silence and reverberated all around them. It went on for long minutes before stopping as abruptly as it had begun.

'Wow,' she said unsteadily into a silence that still echoed with the crack of thunder. Normally the first hint of lightning had her literally cowering under the blankets, and she had never seen anything like that display of ferocious power. She moistened her lips, very glad of Tom's massive, reassuring presence. 'Do you think that's it?'

But that was only the beginning. Before Tom had a chance to reply, the wind was upon them. Like a wild animal, it snarled through the palms, shaking them in savage fury until they bent like saplings. It thrashed its way into the under-growth, whipping the foliage from side to side, and hurled itself at the house.

And then the rain hit them.

Imogen had never seen rain like it. It fell like a wall of water, thundering down onto the veranda roof and hammering into the sand. The noise was deafening, brutal, and she huddled closer into Tom's side.

'All right?' He had to shout over the sound of the rain, but she could still hardly hear him.

She had been watching the rain with a mixture of awe and terror, but at his question she pulled away slightly so that she could look up at him. The silvery eyes gleamed back down at her and she realized, to her astonishment, that the corners of his mouth were turned up. He was actually smiling!

'You're *enjoying* this!'

Tom's smile broadened at the accusing note in her voice. 'I like storms,' he admitted. 'Don't you think this is exciting?'

Now he came to mention it, that *was* excitement quivering along her veins, but it wasn't due to the storm. It was being pressed close into his body, knowing that if she turned her head just a little bit more his throat was only inches away. It would take so little to lean into him and touch her lips to his skin and, once she'd done that, she could blizzard tiny kisses along his jaw to his mouth.

And, if she got that far and he was still smiling, she could find out if his lips were as cool and firm as they looked. She could kiss him the way she had been trying so hard not to think about kissing him all week. She could squirm onto his lap and wind her arms around his neck and perhaps Tom would kiss her back. Perhaps his hands would slide over her, perhaps he would peel off her clothes, perhaps he would take her inside to that big bed and make love to her…

Imogen gulped. Tom was talking about the storm, remember?

'*Exciting* isn't the word I'd use,' she managed.

Tom laughed and pulled her closer. He hadn't meant to, but she fitted so perfectly into him, and she was so soft and so warm and so gorgeous that his arm seemed to tighten of its own accord. The storm was awesome, without a doubt, but the millions of volts crackling across the sky were muted compared to the feeling that jolted through him whenever Imogen shifted slightly and the thin material of her dress beneath his hand slithered over her skin.

Even as he looked down into her face, Tom knew that it was a mistake. The muted glow of the lamp inside was just enough for their eyes to meet, and once they'd snared they were both caught. Tom's smile faded slowly as her gaze held his. He knew just how blue her eyes were, but in this light they were dark and deep and he was drowning in them.

The sound and fury of the storm was forgotten as something undeniable crackled into life between them. Imogen couldn't have looked away if she had tried. It was as if some irresistible force were drawing them together, and her blood drummed with anticipation.

At last—at *last*—he was going to kiss her, and she was going to kiss him back, just as she'd dreamed about. She wasn't going to think about anything except how good it was going to feel. Parting her lips, she lifted her face as Tom lowered his head…

CHAPTER EIGHT

A SUDDEN jagged flash of lightning severed the dark and thunder crashed so terrifyingly close to the house that they both flinched apart in the blinding light. The next moment it was gone and they were plunged into utter darkness.

Imogen stiffened, the old fear clutching at her throat.

'The generator's gone,' Tom yelled in her ear. 'Don't worry. There's a flashlight inside.'

He took his arm from round her and she grabbed him in panic, frantic at the thought of waiting alone in the dark with the storm screaming around her. 'Don't leave me!'

'I'm not going to leave you.' He took firm hold of her hand. 'Come with me. It'll be fine once we get some light.'

Without even a glimmer of starlight, the depth of the darkness was disorientating. Hand in hand, they groped their way to the door and then inside. Tom remembered Ali showing them the flashlight and how to light the gas lamps—for just such an eventuality, he supposed—but it still took some time to find it and, when his hand did finally close on it, he exclaimed with relief.

'At last!'

He clicked it on and they both blinked at the brightness of the beam. To Imogen's relief, the blackness that had been pressing so heavily around them shrank back instantly.

'That's better,' said Tom, and it was, until he looked down to see that he was still holding Imogen's hand. 'Are you OK?' he asked carefully.

She followed his gaze to their linked fingers and a flush crept up her cheeks. 'Yes, I'm fine,' she said, awkwardly disentangling her hand.

Funny, thought Tom. That didn't feel better any more.

He had been so close to kissing her. If that lightning hadn't taken out the electricity just then, he wouldn't have been able to stop himself. And where would that have ended?

Tom knew where. In that bed, and in the very situation he had just managed to convince himself that he should avoid.

Imogen was clearly thinking better of things as well. He had noticed how quickly she had withdrawn her hand from his, and now she was hugging her arms about her nervously. She might still be spooked by the storm, but he thought it was more likely that she was unnerved by the fact that her boss had almost kissed her.

Best to pretend that nothing had happened, he decided.

'Well,' he said, a little too heartily, 'let's light the gas lamps and then we may as well have something to eat. There are plenty of salads in the fridge.'

Imogen never forgot that meal in the hissing light of a gas lamp while the rain crashed onto the roof and her fingers twitched and tingled where they had been curled around Tom's. She couldn't keep her eyes off his lean, solid body, massive and reassuring in the wildness of the dark night.

She tried not to stare, but her eyes kept skittering back to him, only to skitter away again the moment they collided with his pale grey gaze. Not that it mattered where she looked; all she could see were the hard angles of his face, his hands, his mouth. His *mouth*... Had he always had that mouth?

It was just the shadows cast by the lamp, Imogen tried to

tell herself. Just the power of the downpour, the energy of the lightning, that was making her feverish. Just the storm that was raging outside and deep inside her, fizzing like lightning in her blood and making her heart thunder so loudly that if it hadn't been for the rain, Tom must surely have heard it.

It was almost a shock when the rain stopped as abruptly as it had begun. One moment it was pounding down, the next there was an uncanny silence, broken only by the steady drip, drip from the huge tropical leaves outside, before the insects erupted into frenzy and the whole island steamed in the aftermath.

Imogen knew just how it felt. Leaping up, she made a big show of clearing away the plates and putting the food away. Tom hadn't said anything but it was obvious that he had changed his mind about kissing her.

It had been too easy to get carried away by the darkness and the drama of the storm, she reminded herself. And put herself in Tom's position. He was only a man, after all. She had been young, female and alone with him in the dark. Who could have blamed him for being tempted to forget Julia's rejection with someone who was clinging to him like a limpet?

Or for thinking better of it when the lights came on again?

It was just as well nothing had happened, Imogen decided. It would have made it very awkward. Tom was still her boss, and they were going to have to go back to working together in a couple of weeks.

And even if he *had* kissed her, it wouldn't have meant anything. She didn't want to be just a poor substitute for Julia, did she?

Did she?

No, Imogen told herself firmly. Absolutely not. She had narrowly escaped making the most enormous fool of herself, and it wasn't going to happen again. From now on, there would be no holding hands, no pressing herself against him, no fantasising about kissing him. They had agreed to be friends and a friend was all she would be.

Imogen woke the next morning to a bright blue sky. The air was rinsed and sparkling and when they set off for the reef as usual, the water was so still and so clear that it was hard to believe in the ferocity of the storm the night before. If it hadn't been for the intensity of the island scents, heady and lush after the rain, Imogen might have thought it had all been a dream.

She was hoping that excruciating awareness of Tom would turn out to have been a dream too, but if anything it was worse in the diamond-bright light, when every line around his eyes, every crease in his cheek, seemed extraordinarily clear, and when the severe planes and angles of his face were etched against the blue sky.

Remembering her vow, though, Imogen chattered brightly all the way to the reef, and gave what she thought was an excellent impression of a girl too inane to harbour lustful thoughts about her boss.

It was a relief to put on the mask and snorkel, to hide her face in the water and lose herself in the absorbing world beneath the surface. The silence was soothing. There was just the coolness of the water and the sound of her breathing and the fish drifting below in a spectacle of colour, and by the time Tom indicated that they should go back, she was feeling much more herself. She was able to be really normal as the little boat skimmed over the water, and her spirits lifted.

See, she could do this, she congratulated herself as she settled onto the lounger in the sun a little later and opened her book. Last night had been an aberration. She would blame it all on the storm. All she had to do was carry on treating Tom as a friend and enjoy the holiday. She would have to worry about how they got back to a working relationship when they got home.

One thing was sure, she couldn't see them being friends in London. Their lives were just too different. Tom wouldn't be happy slobbing out on the sofa while she and Amanda gossiped, dissected the latest celebrity mags and tested each other on developments in the latest soaps. He wouldn't offer to ring for a takeaway when it turned out there was nothing in the fridge, or want to lie in bed until lunchtime on a Sunday.

And he would never be able to cope with their messy flat, Imogen realised, remembering his need for order and control. He needed someone like Julia—gorgeous, glamorous Julia, who probably drifted around art galleries looking intelligent on Sundays and no doubt lived in an immaculately tidy apartment.

No, they might be friends on Coconut Island, but there was no point in thinking that it could be the same in London.

When Tom appeared with a glass of fresh lime juice a little later, she put her book down with a cheerful smile.

'You make a great barman,' she told him. 'I'll owe you lots of coffees at your desk when we get back to the office.'

No harm in reminding him that she hadn't forgotten reality, no matter how much it must have seemed it the night before when she had clung to him and her eyes had been crawling all over him.

'Actually, it's Ali you should be making the coffee for,' said Tom, sitting sideways on the lounger next to hers. 'He made these. He was just finishing tidying up after the storm when I was checking my email.' He swirled lime juice around his glass with a faint frown. 'Does tonight mean anything to you?'

'No. Should it?'

'He was trying to tell me about something that had been arranged for tonight, but I couldn't get what he was talking about.'

Imogen pulled a face. 'No idea. Perhaps there's a party or

something at the resort? He could have been asking if we wanted to go.'

'God, I hope not,' said Tom in dismay. 'I said yes, OK, just because it seemed easier than trying to understand. But maybe you'd like to go and meet other people?' he added belatedly.

Normally she would have loved the idea of a party, but there was nothing Imogen wanted to do less right then. There were only two weeks left, she had remembered earlier, and she didn't want to share Tom for even a minute of it with anyone else. But she couldn't tell him that in case he thought she was needy and reading too much into what had—or hadn't—happened last night.

'It might be fun,' she said as casually as she could. 'Let's see what happens tonight.'

'Are you dressed?' Imogen heard Tom call from the veranda that evening as she put on her lipstick. 'Ali's here with the boat.'

Just in case it turned out that they were going to a party, Imogen had put on her only smart dress. It was a pale creamy yellow and made of a gorgeous silky material that slithered coolly over her skin and was perfect for putting on after a day in the sun. She had tried to be sensible and sit in the shade as much as possible, but even so the sun had turned her skin to a warm gold and her hair was streaked with blonde. The dress set her new sun-drenched colouring to perfection.

'I wonder what's going on,' she said to Tom, fixing in her earrings as she joined him on the veranda.

'Let's go and see.'

Barefoot like Imogen, Tom led the way down to the jetty. He was browner too, and his silver eyes made an even more startling contrast than usual with his tanned skin. Following him along the jetty, Imogen found her eyes resting hungrily on his back, and she squirmed at the guilty desire that swirled deep inside her like liquid gold.

Stop it, she told herself sternly. Don't look at him. Don't even *think* about it.

Ali was waiting for them in a dinghy at the end of the jetty. All smiles, he gestured out to a beautiful wooden boat waiting beyond a reef.

'For you,' he said.

'It doesn't look like a party anyway,' said Tom in relief.

Imogen was watching the boat. 'Isn't it lovely? It's called a *dhoni*, I think. I remember reading about them when I was booking the island. Apparently they're fabulous for a sunset cruise. I wonder if that's what this is?'

'You didn't book it?'

'No, but it's possible Julia did,' she said slowly. 'She asked me for all the details of the resort at one point. Maybe she was planning a surprise for you?'

'Well, we may as well find out.' Tom pointed at himself and Imogen, and then at the boat with a questioning look at Ali, who nodded vigorously.

'Yes. Come, come.' He waved them towards him.

'He seems to be expecting us,' said Tom. 'What do you want to do? I can tell him there's been a mistake, or we can go along and see what happens.'

'Let's go,' she said. 'It'll be fun.'

The *dhoni* rocked gently as they climbed on board. Tom and Imogen were shown to the prow, which had been laid with luxurious cushions, and they settled down, feeling self-conscious as the crew pulled up the anchor and hoisted the square sail.

Once the sails were up and filled, the engine was cut and there was just the slap and rustle of the waves against the wooden hull. The sea breeze lifted their hair and filled their nostrils with an ocean tang, while the water deepened to a dark, beautiful blue and the setting sun turned the light to gold.

'I don't know whose idea this was, but it was a great one,' said Imogen, thrilled by the lift and fall of the boat.

Tom watched her smiling with pleasure, and his throat ached. She was all warmth and light in the sunset. Her skin was honey-coloured, her hair bleached with sunshine, and the pale yellow dress clung enticingly to her curves and fell in soft folds around her bare legs.

The urge to reach for her, to slide his palm up over her smooth knee, beneath her skirt to explore her thigh, was so strong that he got abruptly to his feet to lean on the side of the boat.

'Dolphins,' he said, pointing, relieved at the distraction.

'Where?' Imogen jumped to her feet to join him. 'Oh, yes! Oh, aren't they *wonderful*?'

Face alight, she leant beside him, her arm only inches from his. She wasn't looking at him. She was watching the dolphins with delight as they played in the frothy wake from the prow, leaping and rolling with effortless grace through the water. A warm breeze blew her hair around her face and she held it back as best she could with one hand.

'This is all perfect.' She sighed, turning to him with a smile.

'Yes,' he said, but he was looking at her rather than the dolphins. 'It is.'

That was when Imogen made the mistake of looking into his eyes, and her smile faltered. It was just like the night before, when at least there had been the excuse of darkness for gazing back at him. Now she had dolphins to watch, the boat to discover, the thrill of the deep, dark ocean and the beauty of the sunset to distract her, and yet she still couldn't wrench her eyes from Tom's silvery-grey ones. They held an expression she had never seen before, one that she couldn't identify but which made her heart kick into a new, slower, reverberating rhythm that sent the blood humming along her veins and lit a tremble of heat deep inside her.

Held together by an invisible skein, neither of them noticed that the sails were being lowered. They were oblivious to the boat turning or Ali readying the dinghy once more, and only a shout from the captain to a member of the crew jerked them back to awareness of where they were.

They both looked quickly away.

Tom cleared his throat. 'What's happening now?'

'I'm not sure. We're stopping for some reason. It's just a sandbar, but there's someone there…' Imogen peered over the beautifully carved wooden rail, not sure whether she was relieved or sorry at the distraction.

So much for all her stern resolutions this morning about putting last night behind her. All it took was one look in Tom's eyes and she was lost. Her pulse was thumping and she felt ridiculously shaky.

'It looks as if we're going ashore,' she said, forcing a smile, but avoiding his gaze. 'I've always wanted to go on a magical mystery tour, haven't you?'

'No,' said Tom, who was way out of his comfort zone. 'I like to know where I'm going.'

But he went readily enough when they were gestured to the dinghy, and then ferried across the translucent shallows to the sandbar. Once there, it seemed obvious that they should get out, so Tom helped Imogen jump onto the sand and looked enquiringly at Ali.

'For you,' he said, pointing them towards a frail elderly man dressed in immaculate white who seemed to be waiting for them.

'What's going on?' Tom muttered out of the corner of his mouth as they headed obediently towards the old man.

'I've got no idea,' confessed Imogen, baffled, but when

they got a bit closer she saw that a circle had been drawn in the sand and she stopped and tugged at Tom's sleeve.

'What is it?'

'I'm getting a bad feeling about this,' she whispered.

Tom glanced at the elderly man and then back at Imogen. He was just an old man, surely? What was so threatening about that?

'I think it might be set up for a wedding ceremony,' she told him.

'*What?*'

Tom's voice rose and she shushed him quickly. 'I read about it when I was finding out about honeymoons here for you. You can't actually get married here because it's a Muslim country, but you can have a special ceremony to bless your marriage or renew your vows.'

'And you booked one?' he asked, aghast.

'Of course not,' hissed Imogen, 'but what if Julia did? She might have thought it would be romantic. There's so much organisation that goes into a wedding, it sometimes seems hard for the bride and groom to really enjoy it and think about what they're promising in the ceremony. This way you'd have had time to relax after the wedding and say your vows again when you could really concentrate on each other.

'I think it's a nice idea,' she finished defiantly, reading the scepticism in Tom's expression without difficulty.

Now Tom thought about it, Julia *had* dropped some cryptic comments about their vows but he hadn't been listening properly. If he had, he would have told her that he couldn't imagine anything worse.

But it was too late for that now. 'If all this was booked in advance, why didn't they tell us anything about it when we arrived?'

'Perhaps they did,' said Imogen, remembering how distracted they had both been at the resort. 'Neither of us were really paying much attention to what the manager was saying.'

'I suppose not. God, what a mess!'

Tom cast a glance at the old man, who smiled encouragingly and beckoned them closer.

'What are we going to do?' asked Imogen in an urgent undertone.

'We'd better bluff it out,' Tom decided. 'It's too difficult to try and explain now. You're sure it's not a legal ceremony?'

'It's just symbolic.'

'There you are,' he said, taking her arm. 'It won't mean anything. Better five minutes of mumbo-jumbo than half an hour of awkward explanations.'

'I don't know…' Imogen hung back, not at all convinced, but Tom was urging her forwards and suddenly she was looking into the old man's face. It was very calm, and his eyes were wise.

'Your name?' he asked her, gesturing her into the circle.

'Imogen.'

'And Tom,' Tom supplied quickly before he was asked and stepped into the circle facing Imogen.

The celebrant nodded. 'You have come to celebrate your love for each other?'

'Er…yes.'

If he was surprised at their hesitation, he didn't show it. 'There are just the two of you. That is good,' he said. 'This is about you and no one else. This is your circle. Stand inside it, share it. It binds you together. It represents oneness—your oneness with each other and with the earth. It represents your love.'

Imogen bit her lip. It felt all wrong to be deceiving him, but it was too late to go back now. It didn't mean anything, she tried to remind herself, but as the old man's gentle words of blessing fell, an invisible net seemed to drop over the circle where she and Tom stood in the sand, drawing the two of them tighter and tighter together and cutting off the rest of the world.

The sun was setting fire to the sea that stretched all around the sandbar. It was an extraordinary, dream-like feeling to stand there in that blazing golden light, to be astonishingly aware of the soft white sand beneath her feet, and of Tom's hands holding hers in a warm, strong clasp.

Imogen didn't want to look at Tom, but she couldn't tear her eyes from his and she found herself hanging on to his hands as if he was all that could keep her anchored in reality.

The ceremony was very simple, and very moving. Held by the silver of Tom's eyes, Imogen heard the old man talking about love, about commitment, about finding completeness together, and every word seemed right.

'Imogen,' he finished at last, 'is this man, Tom, the man you love?'

She swallowed. 'Yes,' she said huskily, and her heart rang with the knowledge that it was true.

'Tom, is this woman, Imogen, the woman you love?'

Tom's voice was steadier than hers. 'Yes.'

'Imogen, take Tom's heart, hold it safe. And, Tom, take the heart Imogen gives you and cherish it. Love each other, be true to each other, find peace in each other. Find joy in each other always.'

Ridiculously, Imogen felt her eyes sting with tears. 'I will.'

'I will,' said Tom after the barest of pauses.

'Promise this with a kiss.'

Imogen's eyes locked with Tom's. She saw something flare in the silver depths, and her breath caught.

He was going to kiss her. Of course he was going to kiss her. He had no choice but to kiss her.

At last—at last!—he was going to kiss her.

The corners of Tom's mouth turned up very slightly as he let go of Imogen's hands to cup her face between his palms.

'I promise,' he said softly, so softly that she wondered if she was even supposed to hear it, and then his mouth touched hers.

His lips weren't cool at all. They were warm and firm and sure and so wickedly exciting that Imogen gave a tiny gasp, taken unawares by the intensity of the response that rocketed through her.

Tom's hands drifted down to slide beneath her hair so that he could cup her head and deepen his kiss, and Imogen's world dissolved into giddy delight as she let herself kiss him back the way she had so longed to do. Leaning into him, she slipped her arms around his waist and held tight to the sweetness of the moment.

It might turn out to be a mistake, she knew, but right then it felt utterly right and she murmured an inarticulate protest when Tom reluctantly broke the kiss and lifted his head.

Both of them had forgotten the old man, who was still standing there, watching them with a faint smile. Still reeling from the kiss they had shared, they barely noticed as he deftly looped their wrists together with a knotted twine made from shredded leaves.

He made a beautiful gesture with his hands. 'It is done,' he said simply and stepped back. 'You are bound together, and now you are one.'

'What have we done?'

All smiles, Ali had escorted them back to the *dhoni*, where Imogen had been greeted with a garland made of frangipani flowers. The heady fragrance was making her feel slightly sick as she and Tom were left alone in the prow at last. Or perhaps it was the way her senses were still spinning from the realisation of how much she loved him?

How much, and how hopelessly.

Now, as the sails unfurled and the boat dipped gently into the swell, Imogen held onto the rail, afraid that her trembling legs wouldn't hold her up any longer.

'We haven't done anything,' said Tom, unfastening the twine around their wrists. He hesitated, just for a moment, and then dropped it into the sea. 'It was a ritual,' he said. 'It didn't mean anything.'

Imogen watched the loop disappear and wanted to cry. It hadn't felt meaningless. 'We made promises,' she said with difficulty.

Tom looked away. She was right. And wasn't he the one who prided himself on always keeping his promises?

It had been the strangest of experiences, standing in that circle with Imogen. He had been feeling exasperated at the whole muddle, Tom remembered, but the moment he'd taken her hands and looked into those blue, blue eyes an inexplicable sense of relief had swept over him, as if, without knowing quite how it had happened, he'd found himself at exactly the right place at exactly the right time, doing just what he'd needed to do.

And then he had kissed her, and her sweetness had made him reel. The taste of her, the feel of her, the softness of her lips and the silkiness of her hair around his hands was still thrumming through him, beating insistently along his veins and making him feel…what? Edgy? Apprehensive? *Excited?*

Surely not.

'It wasn't real,' he said, wishing he didn't sound so much as if he were trying to convince himself. 'We're not really married.'

They couldn't be married. Neither of them wanted to be married. It was ridiculous to think anything had happened on that sandbar.

'No, of course not.' Imogen mustered a smile. 'I can

hardly believe it actually happened, to tell you the truth. It was like a dream.'

'This whole week has been like a dream,' said Tom, coming to join her at the rail. 'It's as if we're in a kind of bubble with no connection to life at home.'

She nodded. 'Yes, that's exactly what it feels like.' She managed another smile, a better one this time. 'It's going to be a shock to wake up when we go home!'

'We don't have to wake up just yet.' Succumbing to temptation, Tom took Imogen's hands and turned her gently to face him. 'We could keep the dream going a little bit longer.'

His fingers were warm and persuasive around hers, and Imogen felt dizzy at his nearness again. 'The dream?' she croaked.

'That we're here because we want to be together,' he said. 'We both know it's not true, and that it couldn't last even if it were. As soon as we get back to London, everything will be different. The dream will be over. We won't be able to get it back, and we won't want to.'

Was he making any sense? Tom wondered. He wasn't sure if he understood himself what he was trying to say to Imogen, and part of him was already wondering if he was making the most terrible mistake. But another, stronger part was urging him on.

'We're not the same people here that we are in London,' he said. 'We want different things at home but here…maybe here we want the same. I know what I want. I want to kiss you again. I want to touch you again. I don't want to spend another night on that damned couch thinking about you alone in the bed and wishing that I could be with you.'

Imogen was looking pole-axed, the blue eyes wide with astonishment. She opened her mouth to speak, but Tom was afraid to hear what she was going to say and he rushed on before she could start.

'I know you're still hung up on Andrew. I know you're hanging out for something perfect that I can't give you, but I was just thinking that while we're here, maybe it *could* be perfect. We both know this isn't real, but we've still got two weeks. Why not make the most of it?'

'You mean as if this really was a honeymoon?' Imogen found her voice at last. 'As if we meant those vows we've just taken?'

'Yes,' said Tom. 'We're not talking about forever,' he added quickly. 'As soon as we get back to London, we can forget about this time. We can pretend it never happened. But for now…now there's just the two of us, and we can…we can love each other, just like we've just promised.' He paused, looking down into her face, trying not to show how desperate he was for her to agree. 'What do you think?'

Imogen's fingers twined around Tom's. *It couldn't last*, he had said. *We're not talking about forever.* She was going to hurt when it was over, when she had to go back to being his PA and greeting him coolly every morning.

But she was going to hurt anyway, Imogen realised. That was what happened when you fell in love with a man like Tom.

It wasn't supposed to be like this. She had wanted the perfect relationship. She wasn't supposed to fall in love with a man who didn't do love, who would give her two weeks and no longer.

But she had done it anyway, and wasn't two weeks better than nothing? At least when they said goodbye, as they would in two weeks' time, she would have some memories to treasure. That would be all she would have, Imogen knew. There was no point in hoping that the dream would last.

Find joy in each other, the celebrant had told them. She could choose that, or she could choose to be sensible.

Imogen chose joy. It would be temporary, like everything else she did, but it would still be joy.

And how else was she to resist him for the next two weeks?

Smiling, she tugged her hands from Tom's to rest them flat against his chest and looked up at him. 'I think it's a very good idea,' she said.

Tom stared at her for a moment, as if hardly daring to believe what she had said, and then his eyes blazed and an answering smile illuminated his face. Sweeping her into his arms, he kissed her fiercely, hungrily, and Imogen melted into him, warm and willing, her fingers clutching at his shirt to stop herself from dissolving with sheer pleasure as the heat washed through her.

Giddy with the glorious relief of being able to kiss each other, touch each other, the way they had wanted to all week, they sank down onto the cushions under the darkening sky, crushing the frangipani garland between them. The fragrance of the creamy yellow flowers enveloped them, while the boat rose and fell, and there was only the shush of water against the hull, the creak of wood and the occasional flap of the sail.

The crew talked quietly at the back, giving Tom and Imogen complete privacy, but they were aware only of each other in any case. Tom's body was hard and heavy as he pressed her into the soft cushions, his hands sliding possessively under the yellow dress.

Imogen wrapped her arms around him and forgot everything else. She was sinking under a tide of heat. Every now and then she would surface, gasping, almost frightened by the need to touch him everywhere, feel him everywhere, and a tiny part of her would wonder if she was making a terrible mistake. But how could it be a mistake when his lips felt this good, when his mouth was this exciting, when his hands were moving over her, tracing wicked patterns of desire, and she was unravelling with the need for more, more, more…?

The stars were out above Coconut Island when they made their way back along the little jetty. Afterwards, Imogen could never remember exactly how they had got there. Ali must have taken them in the dinghy, she supposed, but all she remembered was the feel of the smooth bleached wood beneath her bare feet and the gentle slap of water against the posts. She was preternaturally aware of everything: of the silky dress whispering against her legs, of Tom's warm grip on her hand, of her mouth still tingling, her body still thumping with desire.

It all looked so familiar, she thought as they climbed the veranda steps. It all looked exactly the same when it should be different. Everything had changed since they had walked down these same steps to see Ali waiting for them at the end of the jetty.

Then they had been boss and PA; now they were husband and wife.

CHAPTER NINE

EXCEPT that they weren't, not really. Imogen's steps faltered at the sudden moment of clarity.

Tom was behind her, nuzzling her neck as he guided her through the door and pushed her back against it so that he could kiss her again, his hands hard and urgent. 'What is it?'

'You…you don't think we'll regret this?' she asked unsteadily, trying to hang on to the last shreds of rationality but it was hard when the feel of his lips on her bare shoulder was enough to make her inhale sharply.

'We're going to have to go back to working together,' she reminded him with difficulty as he started kissing his way down her throat. 'How are we going to do that if we…?'

'How are we going to spend the next two weeks if we don't…?' countered Tom, smiling wickedly against her skin. His fingers had found the zip of her dress and were easing it down. 'Let's just forget work for now.'

Imogen shivered at the sureness of his touch. She had a hazy idea that it wasn't going to be as easy as he made out, but she couldn't think, not with his hands sliding over her, not with his mouth devastating the last of her defences, not with the heat pooling deep inside her. It spilt feverishly along her veins until she stopped trying to think at all and gave herself up to the deep, dark spool of desire, to the feel of his mouth and his hands and his lean, hard body.

The bed was wonderfully wide. It was like being cast away, with the deep thrill of knowing that they were completely alone. There was no one to see them, no one to hear them. There was just the two of them, entwined, where nothing mattered but touching and tasting and feeling.

'Let's just think about being here,' whispered Tom in her ear. 'Let's just think about now.'

And so Imogen closed her mind to the future and did just that.

The days that followed stayed forever golden in Imogen's memory. At one level, things went on much as they had done before. In the mornings they explored the reef, while afternoons were spent on the beach, swimming, reading or just lying in the shade and talking.

Often Imogen was content just to sit and gaze at the sea, marvelling at the intensity of the light, of the blueness and the greenness and the pristine whiteness of the beach. She would inhale slowly, savouring the wonderfully clean, invigorating smell of sea and sunlight, feeling the heat in her nose, watching the way the breeze made the palms sway and sent their tattered shadows dancing over skin and sand.

She had never seen things so clearly before, had never been intoxicated by smell and touch and taste the way she was now. It was as if all her senses were supercharged with Tom at her side.

The laptop lay unopened now, as Tom succumbed to the dream-like atmosphere of the island. He liked to get up early in the morning, when Imogen was still asleep, and walk down to the jetty, when the light was pearly and the lagoon was quiet and still.

Imogen preferred the early evening. She loved washing off

the tingling, salty feeling of too much sea and too much sun, and changing into something loose and comfortable. Tom would have made a cool drink by then, and they sat on the veranda together, watching the sun set. A hush fell over the island then, and in silence they watched the sky flush pink, deepening with astonishing speed to a blaze of orange and scarlet, while the sea shimmered and they both remembered standing on the sandbar, promising to love each other for ever in the same glowing light.

Once it had faded, the tropical night dropped with a speed Imogen could never get used to. It was the signal for the cicadas to start whirring and they would sit on, waiting for the bats to come swooping past the veranda and spotting the little geckos that darted up the walls.

Imogen wished they could stay on Coconut Island for ever. She loved the colours, the smell of the dried coconut husks on the beach, the hot wind that soughed through the trees and ruffled the surface of the lagoon.

Most of all, she loved being with Tom. She loved the long sweet nights, the mornings when he returned from his walk to wake her with drifting hands, the afternoons in the shade. She loved every moment when he touched her, every second that she could reach out for him and find him there.

But beneath the pleasure she took in every moment lurked the knowledge that it couldn't last. Imogen tried desperately to forget that this time would pass but, just when she least needed a reminder, some stern, sensible part of her brain would put up its hand and point out that the days were passing and that before too long she would have to go back to the greyness of London in March. Back to the squash of commuters on the Tube, coats steaming with rain, back to dripping umbrellas and Monday mornings. Back to being Tom's PA.

There would be no more nights together, no more lazy afternoons.

No more loving.

Imogen would push the thought away, but the days passed in relentless succession and suddenly it was their last evening on Coconut Island.

Leaning on the veranda railing next to Tom, she watched the sun setting in a blaze of crimson behind the reef.

I'm not ready, she wanted to cry. *I can't face this yet.*

But she would have to find a way to face it, and to reassure Tom that she hadn't forgotten what they had agreed.

She turned her glass between her fingers. 'Funny to think this is the last time we'll do this,' she said.

It was the last time they would watch the sun set together. The last time they would sit in the dark and watch the bats swoop and dive. The last time they would listen to the insects ratcheting up their whirring, creaking, rasping chorus.

The last time they would make love in that big bed.

She had known this time would come, Imogen reminded herself, squaring her shoulders. It wasn't as if it was a surprise. She had known all along that it would come to this.

'This time tomorrow we'll be back in London.'

'Yes,' said Tom heavily.

He ought to be glad. He would be going back to the office, back to where everything was straightforward and he knew where he was. He would be in control of his life again, not like here.

It was different here. The sun and the sea and the quietness had worn down his defences, and he had forgotten the lessons he had learnt so carefully—to guard his feelings, to keep control. He had let himself relax and lose himself in Imogen. It had felt so right at the time but now Tom was beginning to wonder if he had made a terrible mistake.

At the time, it had seemed a sensible idea. Why spend another two weeks feeling frustrated when they could come to an agreement as two consenting adults? It was all going to be so easy. They had a definite time limit. There would be no awkward discussions about when or how to say goodbye. The two weeks would end, and it would be over. Simple as that.

But he hadn't counted on how quickly he would get used to Imogen, to her laughter and her warmth and the wild, un-expected passion that had ensnared them both.

He hadn't counted on the way his body would crave hers like this. He had always been so controlled, and yet now he had this constant urge to touch her, to slide his hands over her and taste the sun and the salt on her skin, to feel her smile against his throat.

He wouldn't be able to do that any more.

Tom tried to tell himself that it would be fine, that he would have work to distract him, but whenever he tried to imagine sleeping without Imogen's softness curved into him, or waking early in the morning and not being able to turn to her, he felt something twist uncomfortably deep inside him and a bleakness crept into his chest.

'Perhaps it will all feel different when we get home,' he said, hoping that it was true.

'I'm sure it will,' said Imogen brightly. 'It's been lovely, but we both know it's not real. Real will be going into work on Monday morning, and dealing with everything that's happened while we've been away. We'll be too busy to remember anything but the fact that I'm your PA and you're my boss.'

She seemed very confident, thought Tom, but why wouldn't she be? They had made a deal that this would be a time out of time. He could hardly blame her if that was how she was treating it. It had been his idea, after all.

The sunset was as spectacular as ever, but Tom didn't even

see it. He was confused and uneasy at the way everything was slipping out of control. How had it happened? When had he started to *feel* like this?

It had been easy when he was with Julia. He had known exactly where he was and what he wanted. But with Imogen… The truth was that Tom had never felt the way he did now. Intellectually, he could see that she was the last kind of woman he should fall in love with, but somewhere along the line she had become essential to him in a way he couldn't define. All he knew was that after living with her, laughing with her, loving with her, the thought of life without her made him feel inutterably bleak.

If this was love, Tom didn't like it.

This wasn't the joyous feeling Imogen had described. It was the gut-wrenching sensation of standing on the edge of an abyss.

And what if it *wasn't* love? Tom didn't trust this new feeling. It was too uncomfortable, too unfamiliar. He certainly didn't trust it enough to say anything to Imogen. Less than a month ago, he had been sure that he wanted to marry Julia. Why would Imogen believe that he had changed his mind so completely? Tom wasn't even sure that he believed it himself.

Hadn't they been clear right from the start that this was just a temporary thing? They were making the most of things, no more than that. What they had found together wasn't important. It wasn't something that could last.

No, he couldn't say anything, he had decided. If he blurted out that he was in love with her, he would embarrass her, and if it turned out that he didn't once they got home, he would hurt her, and Tom couldn't bear the thought of that.

And, of course, if he did say something, Imogen might say no. She might reject him, and Tom wasn't sure that he could handle that either. Not again.

The truth, he acknowledged to himself, was that he didn't

dare say anything. He couldn't risk everything he was on feelings that he wasn't sure about. And so he had been imperceptibly distancing himself over the last two or three days. Better to wait until they were home, he convinced himself, and he could tell whether these strange new feelings were real or just part of this fantasy place.

Imogen had picked up on his subtle withdrawal and had drawn her own conclusions. Tom was already thinking about going home, about working together again, she decided. Was he trying to find the words to remind her that what they had was only ever intended to be temporary? She would have to make things easy for him. He would be dreading a conversation where feelings might be mentioned.

She wasn't looking forward to it herself, but it had to be done. They couldn't just leave and not acknowledge what the last three weeks had been like, but she would have to make it clear that she understood completely that tomorrow it would be over.

Tom still had the fallout from his engagement to Julia to face on his return. He would be preoccupied with that and with work. If she told him how desperately she had fallen in love with him it would just make him acutely uncomfortable. He didn't need that to deal with as well.

No, the best thing she could do for him was to get back to normal as soon as possible; the best thing she could do for herself was to stop fooling herself there could ever be any future in it and make a new life for herself.

The best thing for both of them would be to pretend that these last three weeks had never happened.

Imogen set her glass on the railing, put on a big smile and turned to face Tom properly.

'It's been so wonderful,' she told him. 'I'll never forget this time we've spent together, Tom. It's going to be hard getting used to travelling in less than the lap of luxury, but whenever I get to a beach or see a palm tree, I'll think of you.'

Whenever she closed her eyes or felt the sun on her face or lay in the dark, she would think of him.

She would think of him with every breath, miss him with every beat of her heart.

Tom eyed her broodingly over the top of his glass. 'You still want to go travelling then?'

'Of course.' Imogen kept her smile bright. 'Even more so now, in fact. Being here has given me a real taste for travel.'

She turned back to look out at the lagoon. There was a crimson line along the horizon where the sun had finally disappeared, and the darkness was closing in. The bats would be out any minute now.

'I may not find anywhere as perfect as this, but there will be other beautiful places,' she said.

Places without Tom.

A silence fell. The shrilling of the insects was very loud as it stretched and stretched, until neither could stand it any longer. Inevitably, they both spoke at the same time.

'Imogen—'

'Do you—'

Both stopped awkwardly.

'You first,' said Imogen.

'I just wanted to say…well, it's going to be hard to talk about this when we get back,' said Tom 'It's probably better if we don't, if we just pretend this time never happened, but I want you to know that I'm grateful for everything you've done.'

'You don't need to thank me,' said Imogen. 'I've had a wonderful time.'

'Really?'

'Really,' she said and, as their gazes locked and held, Tom reached out and drew her towards him.

'I'll miss you,' he confessed.

'I'll miss you too,' she whispered, her arms sliding round his neck. 'It's hard to believe that this time tomorrow this will all be over.'

Tom bent his head to find her mouth. 'It's not over yet.'

Imogen swallowed hard as the plane descended through the grey clouds above Heathrow. This was it. The end of blue skies, the end of bright light, the end of the dream.

They had had one last bittersweet night of loving, but that morning they had dressed in silence. Tom had put on his suit again for the journey back. Imogen was wearing the jeans and top that she had travelled out in. After all this time in little more than a sarong, the clothes felt heavy and constricting and her sandals were awkward to walk in.

When Ali had appeared with the dinghy to take them back to the resort, Tom had helped her into the boat for the first stage of that long, inexorable journey. It would be the last time he touched her.

Imogen felt like a snail being torn from its shell, wrenched away from the island, away from the warm blue ocean, dragged across the skies when, with every fibre of her being, she longed to be back under the coconut palms, sitting next to Tom and watching the breeze ruffle the still surface of the lagoon.

Tom was sitting beside her on the plane, but there the similarity ended. They had spoken little on the long flight. His face was set in grim lines, just as it had been on the journey out, and, sensing his withdrawal, Imogen lifted her chin and withdrew in her turn.

He needn't be afraid that she was going to cling, she told herself. She had no intention of embarrassing him by telling him how much she loved him. That hadn't been part of the deal at all. Tom Maddison wasn't the only one who kept his promises.

Down, down into the cloud cover sank the plane and Imogen's heart sank with it. Staring out of the window, she felt a pang as the last of the bright blue sky linking them to the Indian Ocean disappeared and the light dulled and it was just London in March, grey and overcast.

Then it was all happening too fast. They were first off the plane, their baggage appeared quickly and they were heading through Customs before Imogen had a chance to think about how she was going to say goodbye to Tom, before she could find a way to pretend that her heart wasn't breaking.

She tried to stall, wishing frantically that time would somehow slow down, but Tom was already striding onwards, eager, it seemed, to get back to real life. He paused at the exit, his hard gaze sweeping over the crowd in the Arrivals Hall until he identified his driver.

'There's Larry.' He headed towards him. 'He should have the car waiting just outside. Where would you like to go?'

'Actually,' said Imogen, hanging back, 'I think I'll get the Tube.'

Tom frowned. 'It'll be much quicker in a car at this time of day.'

'It's not that.' She forced a smile. 'I think I need to start getting back to normal,' she tried to explain. 'I've had three weeks of lovely luxury, but that's not my life. The next time I'm at an airport, I'll have a backpack and the cheapest ticket I can get.'

Her bag was slipping from her shoulder and she hoisted it back, keeping her smile firmly in place. 'I may as well get used to it now.'

Panic gripped Tom by the throat. He had spent the flight planning how to say goodbye. He couldn't do it on the plane, with flight attendants hovering the whole time. There were too many other people at the baggage carousel. The back of the car would be their only chance for any privacy, he had decided, but now Imogen wanted to say goodbye there and then in the middle of the busy terminal and the careful words he had prepared were promptly wiped from his memory.

'Whatever you like,' he said stiffly instead.

That reference to travelling had obviously been designed to remind him that she had plans that didn't include him. Perhaps it was just as well they would say goodbye here. God only knew what would have come tumbling out if they had been alone in the back of the car with him trying to keep his hands off her.

'So…' Imogen lifted her arms a little helplessly and dropped them back to her sides '…I guess this is it.'

'Yes,' said Tom. There was a sharp ache in the back of his throat. 'I guess it is.'

'See you on Monday, then?'

He nodded. 'Have a good weekend.'

'You too. Well…bye, boss.' From somewhere Imogen produced a brilliant smile, then she turned and walked away towards the signs for the Underground.

'Goodbye, Imogen.'

Tom stood in the busy concourse with the crowds surging around him and watched her go, and felt bleaker than he ever had in his life. He wanted to run after her, to stop her going through the ticket barrier, to drag her onto the next plane to the Maldives.

But he couldn't do that. Imogen had her own life, her own plans, and she had made it very clear that they didn't include him. She was off to see the world. That was what she wanted, what she needed to do. She was young, beautiful, outgoing. Why would she stay with a man like him—older, driven, a self-confessed workaholic?

He was no fun, Tom knew. He had always been too busy

striving for success to be distracted by fun. Imogen deserved someone who would cherish her gaiety and ability to live in the moment. She deserved better than him.

He was better off on his own, anyway, Tom decided, making a determined effort to shake off the sickeningly empty feeling. He couldn't manage this relationship business. He had tried commitment with Julia, and look what had happened! Failure and humiliation.

He wasn't risking rejection again. He might miss Imogen a bit when she went, but he would get just as used to the new PA eventually, and she wouldn't distract him the way Imogen did now. It wasn't as if he and Imogen could ever have had anything in common, Tom reminded himself. They were too different. It could never have lasted.

No, Tom thought as he turned to find his driver, it was all for the best.

Imogen tugged at her jacket as she watched the lift doors close. Her suit felt heavy and uncomfortable, and her feet were cramped in the unfamiliar shoes.

It had been a long weekend. She had smiled and smiled when she'd got into the flat, but Amanda hadn't been fooled for a minute.

'I *knew* this would happen! You're in love with him, aren't you?'

Imogen opened her mouth to deny it and then admitted defeat. 'Yes,' she admitted, 'I am.' But her voice cracked and, in spite of herself, her brave smile wavered and collapsed miserably. 'But it's hopeless, I know that. He doesn't want me now.'

It didn't take long for Amanda to get the whole story out of her. 'I don't think you should give up so easily, Imo,' she said when Imogen had finished and was scrubbing her wet cheeks with a tissue. 'It sounds to me as if this Tom wanted you just as much as you wanted him.'

'That was on the island. He made it very clear that it was just a temporary thing.'

Amanda sniffed. 'Hmm, well, in my experience, it's not what men *say* that matters, it's what they *do*, and he wouldn't have been sleeping with you unless that's what he wanted. It's all very well to decide that you're going to forget it ever happened, but it'll be a very different matter when you're working together. If you're going to be remembering what it was like, chances are that he's going to be doing the same.'

Was it possible? Imogen wondered. Could Tom be missing her too? Or had he already filed her mentally under 'finished business'? He had emotions, she knew, but he kept them locked tightly away, the way he had learnt to do ever since he was a small boy, learning that his mother wasn't coming back. It would be too much to expect him to suddenly get in touch with his feelings, or to assume that those feelings might be about her. It wasn't that long since he had been hurt by Julia, after all.

But…

But perhaps Amanda was right and she shouldn't give up all hope, Imogen began to think tentatively. Surely Tom couldn't have kissed her like that, made love to her like that, if he didn't feel *anything* for her? He had never actually said what he felt, but the physical connection between them had been real enough.

She missed him dreadfully. She missed his lovely, solid male body next to hers. She missed the sound of his voice, reverberating over her skin. She missed the smile in his eyes when he drew her to him.

If she could have that again, might that not be enough? Imogen wondered as she lay achingly alone in her bed. If she could hold him again, feel him again, this awful ache might not be so bad. Tom might not be ready to fall in love, but perhaps he would consider continuing the arrangement they had had on the island...

The idea slid into Imogen's mind and stayed there, impossible to dislodge. But why *wouldn't* it work? she reasoned. She wouldn't ask for commitment. She wouldn't expect him to tell her he loved her. All she wanted was to be with him.

She couldn't blurt it out, of course. Tom would be horrified if she went all emotional on him. She would have to see what he was like on Monday, but if he had missed her a fraction of the way she had missed him, perhaps there was a chance...

It was enough to set Imogen's blood fizzing at the thought of seeing him again as the lift slid upwards. She was sharing it with two others and, although she only recognized them enough to smile, she was burningly aware of their interested glances. They obviously knew exactly who she was.

She had already had a taste of the speculation rife in the office about what she and Tom had got up to while they had been away. The girls on the reception desk had welcomed her back, exclaimed over her tan and clearly not believed a word of her insistence that it had been no more than a business trip.

There would be more of that to come, Imogen knew. Perhaps she should wait until the intense interest had died down before she said anything to Tom about resuming the relationship they had had on the island. She certainly wouldn't embarrass him by acting all doe-eyed around him.

In fact, she should make it clear that she was sticking to their agreement to pretend that nothing had happened until she had some sense of what Tom himself wanted.

Still, her heart hitched in anticipation as she nodded goodbye to the others, stepped out of the lift and hurried along the opulent corridor to her office. The trouble was that she had been thinking too much. Better to just go in and be herself, instead of preparing what she would say. She hadn't had to prepare on Coconut Island, so why start now?

But, after all that, Tom wasn't in his office. Bitterly disappointed, Imogen sat at her desk and spun slowly in the chair.

It felt odd to be back. The island still seemed real, and all this a not wholly comfortable dream. She looked at her watch. This time the week before they had been snorkelling. She had a sudden vivid picture of Tom surfacing beside her, pulling off his mask, flicking the water out of his hair and smiling at her. The sunlight bouncing off the water had thrown a rocking pattern over his skin, and his eyelashes had been dark and spiky and a startling contrast to the silver-grey eyes.

The memory pierced Imogen like a skewer and she swung her chair back to face her desk and switched on her computer. Distraction, that was what she needed.

Her inbox was dauntingly full. It was a long time since she had last checked her email on Coconut Island, since Tom had pushed his laptop aside and suggested a swim instead. Imogen could still feel the delicious coolness of the lagoon as she sank into the wa—

But she wasn't supposed to be wallowing in those memories. She caught herself up guiltily and scowled at the computer screen as she forced herself to concentrate. Working doggedly through the messages, she did so well that she didn't even notice that Tom had arrived and was watching her from the doorway.

It had been the longest weekend of Tom's life. He had spent it in his sterile apartment, trying to work out what was so different now and, when he did, it came as a shock.

He was lonely.

Tom was furious with himself. He had *never* been lonely. On the contrary, he'd always felt most comfortable on his own, but now...now he was used to Imogen being there. He missed her sweetness and her warmth, and without it he felt cold and somehow empty.

He told himself that he just needed a couple of days to adjust. He thought that he *had*, but the sight of Imogen at her desk left him feeling literally gutted, as if a great fist had reached inside him and wrenched out his entrails.

Engrossed in her emails, she looked composed and unfamiliar, as if she had never laughed in the sunshine, never rolled on top of him and let her hair tickle his bare chest, never teased him with soft kisses.

Never stood on that sandbar and promised to love him for ever.

The suit, the hair pulled back from her face, the air of efficiency all spelt a clear message. She was sticking to the agreement they had made. She was pretending that the past three weeks had never happened and that she was just his PA once more.

He should be grateful, Tom knew. Imogen was making things easy for him. This was his chance to step back and decide how he really felt, but all he could think was that she was making it impossible for him to stride over to the desk, yank her up and into his arms and kiss her the way he really wanted.

That would be madness, of course. It would be a ridiculous, rash, *risky* way to carry on. It would mean he had lost control altogether, and control was all he had to hang on to at the moment.

So in the end all he did was wish her a good morning from the safe distance of the doorway.

Imogen's head jerked up and Tom was momentarily comforted by the blaze of expression in her blue eyes, but it was so quickly veiled that he wondered if he had imagined it just because he wanted to see it so much.

'Good morning,' she replied with some constraint. 'Did you have a good weekend?'

Her cool politeness sent ice creeping over Tom's heart. It was just as well he hadn't grabbed her and kissed her.

'Yes, thank you,' he replied, equally polite, equally cool. There was no point now in confessing to Imogen that he had spent his entire time missing her. 'And you?'

'Fine, thanks,' lied Imogen.

There was an awkward pause.

'You're in early,' said Tom eventually.

'I wanted to get on with things,' she said. 'There's lots to do.'

CHAPTER TEN

THE memory of the island was thundering around the room but Imogen wasn't going to be the first to mention it. What could she say, anyway? *Oh, remember how we lay on the beach and looked at the stars? Remember how it felt to hold hands and feel as if the earth was turning beneath us? Remember how we made love right there and then had to shower off all the sand before we went to bed?*

So she smiled coolly without quite meeting his eyes and handed him a folder. 'These are the most urgent messages.'

Daunted by her composure, Tom took the folder but didn't open it. 'Have you still got the key to Julia's flat?' he asked abruptly.

'I should have.' Imogen rummaged in her drawer. She had used the key when she had returned the wedding presents before they'd left for Coconut Island. 'Yes, here it is,' she said, producing the key and forcing her mind away from the island. Stupid how it took so little for the memories to come swirling back. 'Do you need it back?'

'I was wondering if you could do a job for me,' said Tom, and she assembled a smile from somewhere.

'That's what I'm here for.'

'I spoke to Julia at the weekend,' he told her. 'It turns out that Patrick is going to work in some out-of-the-way place in South America, and Julia's going with him. I can't see her lasting out there,' he admitted, 'but she seems determined to start a new life.

'She hasn't got time to come back to London and sort out the apartment before she goes,' he went on, 'and the agents need it to be cleared so that they can let it again. She just took a small bag with her when she went off with Patrick and, although she hadn't moved everything over here, there will still be some clothes and other stuff left. She says she doesn't want any of it,' Tom finished, 'so she asked if I would get rid of anything that's there. It can all go to charity or the dump.'

Imogen ached at the distant note in Tom's voice. Talking to Julia must have been difficult for him, she knew. He had told her that he didn't love Julia, and Imogen believed him, but she knew how much the other woman's rejection had hurt his pride. Imogen had found it hard settling back into normal life, but how much harder must it be for Tom, who had had to return to an empty flat and the reminder that the perfect life he had planned with Julia had fallen apart?

'Would you like me to deal with that for you?' she said, anticipating his request.

'Thank you,' said Tom.

His formality broke Imogen's heart but she kept her smile in place. 'I'll get on with it as soon as I can.'

In fact, it wasn't until after work that Thursday that Imogen had time to get to the exclusive apartment Julia had rented in Chelsea.

It had been a very long four days, and Imogen was exhausted with the effort of keeping a smile on her face and parrying the not-so-subtle questions of her colleagues, who were desperate to know more about the time she had spent with Tom. Which was hard when she was just as desperate *not* to think about it.

She and Tom had both been careful to avoid any reference to Coconut Island. Inevitably, the atmosphere in the office was strained, but Imogen didn't think they had been doing too badly until one of their senior shareholders had come to see Tom earlier that afternoon. When the meeting was over, Tom had walked him out to Imogen's office and helped him on with his coat while he'd continued to complain about protection orders.

'The world's run mad.' He snorted. 'Next thing we know, flies and slugs will have protection orders! Last year we had bats roosting in the roof and we weren't allowed to get rid of them! Absolutely ridiculous,' he grumbled. 'Bats, I ask you! Horrible little things. Have you ever seen them?'

Over his shoulder, Tom's eyes met Imogen's. 'Yes, I have' was all he said, but it was as if they were both transported back to the veranda on Coconut Island, to the hot tropical dusk and the bats darting and diving in the air. Imogen could practically feel the chair beneath her thighs, almost smell the frangipani drifting through the darkness, and hear the insects whirring and chirruping.

She knew Tom was remembering too. She could see it in the silver-grey eyes as their gazes locked and there was just the two of them, held in thrall by the memory of those long, sweet evenings.

'Well, I'd better get on,' the shareholder was saying, digging in his pockets for his gloves. 'Good to see you again, Tom. Oh, and by the way, I meant to say that I was very sorry to hear about that business in February,' he added gruffly.

'Business?' Tom sounded distracted.

'Your wedding…most unfortunate.' He was obviously embarrassed at having to be specific.

'Oh, that…yes…thank you.'

Imogen was thinking about that exchange as she put the key in the lock and let herself into Julia's apartment.

Tom hadn't said anything when he'd come back from escorting the shareholder to the lift but something had changed with that meeting of their eyes, Imogen was convinced, and she hugged the possibility to her. Perhaps she didn't need to despair, after all.

Wandering from room to room in Julia's gorgeous flat, Imogen let herself dream. Maybe she would go into the office tomorrow and be talking about work when Tom would throw the file they were discussing onto the desk and say he couldn't bear it without her any more. He would sweep her into his arms and tell her she was the one he really wanted. He'd beg her to marry him and stay with him for ever.

Even if he didn't tell her that he loved her, it would be enough, Imogen decided. A man like Tom couldn't suddenly pull all his emotions out of a hat, but there *had* been a chemistry between them, and today it had seemed as if it was still there. They could build on that. She could teach him how to love. She didn't care as long as they could be together.

They could live somewhere like this. Imogen loved this apartment. It had lots of space and light, with a wonderful view of the Thames. She couldn't help comparing it with the flat she shared with Amanda. There was nothing wrong with that, but it was very small and a bit shabby. They had fun there, of course, but this was the kind of place you lived in when you were grown up, when you had made a success of your career and were going to marry a man like Tom.

Dreamily, Imogen opened the wardrobe in the bedroom. Julia hadn't spent much time in London, but it was still full of beautiful clothes. Imogen whistled soundlessly as she checked the labels. Amanda would be wild with envy. This lot ought to raise a lot of money for some lucky charity shop.

Fantasising all the while about living there with Tom, Imogen folded the outfits carefully and put them on the bed, ready to be packed into boxes for collection. She would have to deal with Julia's wedding dress separately. It was hanging in a gorgeous cover behind the door and was much too big to fit in any of the boxes.

Imogen couldn't resist having a look at it. Drawing down the zip, she let out an involuntary sigh of longing. It was exquisite. Very gently she touched the shimmering ivory fabric, marvelling at the detail in the delicately beaded design. Julia had sent her a sketch of the design, but she hadn't realised how beautiful it would be when was made up. This was the wedding dress every girl dreamed of, a dress that would make you look like a princess—gorgeous and utterly romantic.

Lifting it down, she drew off the cover and held the dress up against her, imagining wearing it at her own wedding.

She was walking down the aisle on her father's arm in the village church. He was bursting with pride, her mother was sniffing into a handkerchief, her brothers were rolling their eyes but happy for her anyway. Amanda was there too, ready to step up and take her bouquet when the moment came.

Imogen could practically feel the stone floor beneath her feet and smell that mixture of musty kneeling cushions, old hymn books and wooden pews worn smooth by generations.

In her mind, she looked towards the altar and there was Tom, looking devastating in an austere morning suit. For a moment, she wondered if it could possibly be true, but then the stern features softened as he turned to watch her coming up the aisle, and he smiled at her, the silvery-grey eyes alight with love…

Reluctantly, Imogen wrenched herself from the dream and stroked the beautiful dress longingly. What would it be like to wear a dress like this?

Find out.

The thought slid insidiously into her head and lodged there. Why *not* try it on, after all? It wasn't her dress…but Julia didn't want it. What harm could it do, just to see what she would look like as a bride?

Imogen dithered, then made up her mind. Quickly, she pulled off her clothes and examined the dress in her bra and knickers. Unzipping it carefully, she stepped into the skirt and pulled up the bodice in front of the mirror. The heavy silk felt gorgeous against her skin.

Smiling at her reflection, Imogen reached for the side zip—and the dream promptly shattered under the crashing fist of reality.

There was no way this zip was ever going to do up with her inside it.

Imogen watched her smile wiped out by a wash of humiliation, and a blotchy tide of embarrassed colour surged up her throat. There might as well have been a crowd of spectators, pointing and jeering.

What had she been *thinking*? She knew how slender and elegant Julia was. She had to be a good three sizes bigger than Tom's erstwhile fiancée. Of *course* she wasn't going to fit into Julia's dress.

Of course she wasn't going to fit into Julia's life.

Because that was what she really wanted, Imogen realised dully. She wanted to be slim and sophisticated and beautiful and clever and the kind of woman Tom really wanted to share his life. But she wasn't any of those things. She had to face reality, and the reality was that Tom Maddison was out of her league. He was never going to love her. If he couldn't love Julia, he couldn't love anyone, and she would be fooling herself if she let herself believe otherwise.

And Imogen needed to be loved. That had been the dream, she understood now. It wasn't the wedding, or the dress. It was that moment of looking at Tom and believing that he loved her.

Well, it wasn't going to happen, and she had to accept

that. No matter what she told herself about chemistry, it wouldn't be enough.

A fantasy, Tom had called it. Well, maybe it was, but Imogen knew that nothing else would do. *I'm not prepared to settle for anything less than love*, she had told him, and she was right. She had thought that she could compromise, but she couldn't.

Miserably, she stepped out of the dress and put it back on its hanger, before carrying it over to lay it on the pile destined for the charity shop. Someone was going to get a fabulous bargain.

But it wasn't going to be her.

'That's it for now.' Imogen closed her notebook and got to her feet. 'Except…' she fished in a folder for a piece of paper and passed it across the desk to Tom '…I thought you would like to see the job description I've prepared.'

'Job description?'

'For your new PA.'

Tom felt as if she had reached across the desk and slapped him.

'You're leaving?'

'I told you that I was planning to travel.'

'I thought you said June?' The words felt unwieldy in his mouth and he had to force himself to take the sheet of paper.

'I've advanced my plans a bit,' said Imogen. 'I've got a great deal on a flight to Australia leaving in a month.'

A *month*? Tom felt sick. She obviously couldn't wait to get away.

He stared at the job description, but the words danced in front of his eyes. He should have expected this, he knew. It wasn't as if she hadn't told him very clearly that she wanted to travel. Now he felt a fool for letting himself hope that she would want to stay after all.

It had been stupid of him to even think about trying to find a way back to how things had been on the island.

He had wanted to be careful, knowing that it would be a mistake to rush into anything. Even if Julia's desire to rush into marriage hadn't taught him a lesson, Tom needed to be sure about what he felt. Imogen wasn't like any other girl-friend he had ever had. She didn't fit into his life the way Julia had. She was disturbing, distracting. She had thrown him into turmoil and made him question everything he'd ever thought he wanted. Tom didn't like the way it left him feeling churned up and out of control.

There had been part of him hoping that this feeling would pass. He didn't want to hurt Imogen by telling her that he wanted her, and then realising that he didn't. Tom knew what it was like to be messed around, and he wasn't going to do to Imogen what Julia had done to him.

It was just as well he hadn't said anything, Tom decided. Imogen had obviously been making her own plans, and it would have been awkward for her to find a kind way to let him down. At least this way he would be spared the humiliation of having his feelings thrown back in his face.

This way, he hadn't risked exposing himself only to be left again.

It was probably all for the best, in fact.

'That looks fine,' he said and handed the job description back to Imogen, not having read a word of it. 'Pass it on to HR and tell them it's urgent. I want someone in place before you go.'

Imogen took a final look around her office. No, not hers. It had only ever been temporary, like everything else in her life. She had a temporary job, a temporary relationship on the island, and now she was going off on a temporary trip. When she came back, Imogen vowed, she was going to settle and make something permanent.

But the only permanence she wanted was Tom. The last month had been horrible. Oh, she had put a good face on it. She had smiled and pretended that she was looking forward to her trip. She had told herself that once she got to Australia everything would feel different, but that was what she had told herself after Coconut Island, wasn't it?

Imogen didn't believe it now. She knew that wanting Tom didn't get easier, that loving him didn't get any less. Her memories of the island were no less vivid now than they had been the day after they came back. She couldn't bear the thought of leaving him, but she couldn't bear to stay. Much better to face reality. It would be all too easy to waste her life hoping for the impossible.

What was the point of hankering after a man who didn't know how to love? She might love Tom, but he could never make her happy. She needed to love someone who would love her back, who needed her the way she needed him, and that someone wasn't Tom.

For the past month he had been distant and their conversation largely limited to work, although every now and then he had asked after her plans, as if to underline the fact that he was perfectly happy with her going. He had appointed a new PA, a coolly efficient woman called Judy with impressive qualifications and tons of high-level experience, who would suit Tom perfectly. He wouldn't miss *her* at all.

Facing reality hurt.

'Come on, Imogen, we're all waiting for you.' Sue from HR was beckoning from the door. 'You can't be late for your own farewell party.'

'I've never had a party when leaving a temp job before,' said Imogen as they made their way down to one of the conference rooms. She was baffled by the fuss everyone was making. 'I've only been here a few months.'

'It feels like longer,' said Sue. 'We're all going to miss you. Wait until you see the turnout!'

Imogen's throat tightened when she saw how many people had come to say goodbye and wish her well. She smiled shakily. 'Stop being so nice! You're going to make me wish I wasn't leaving.'

'Oh, yes, of course you'd rather stay here with us than go to Australia!'

There was much good-natured envy of her travels. Imogen plastered on a big smile and agreed that she was incredibly lucky, but all the time she was aware that Tom wasn't there. He had had to go to a meeting, but he had said that he would be back in time for her farewell party.

Imogen dreaded saying goodbye to him, but perhaps it would be better to do it in front of everyone else. An audience might stop her making a complete fool of herself.

'Where's the boss?' grumbled Neville from Finance. 'We can't start the party until he's done the speech.'

'We can't start the party until he's gone,' said someone else. 'He's not exactly a bundle of fun, is he?'

Imogen wanted to tell them they didn't know what he was really like, but there had been more than enough interest in her relationship with Tom. She was fairly sure that a lot of those there were hoping that there would be some juicy titbit of gossip in his speech.

'Here he is now,' she heard someone say, and she turned to see Tom filling the doorway, looking stern and massive and gorgeous. Imogen's heart ripped at the sight of him. How did he do that? All he had to do was stand there and look like that, and her breath caught and longing snarled in her like barbed wire.

Across the room his eyes met hers for a long, jarring

moment, then he was looking away, inclining his head to hear something the Director of HR was saying. He nodded, and then stepped up onto a dais at the front of the room.

Imogen was being nudged forward too. She knew what to expect. She had been to enough excruciating farewell bashes. There would be an awkward speech, the presentation of a jokey present and a gift token of some kind, and then it would be her turn to make a speech. Well, there was nothing to be done but hope that it was over as soon as possible.

But what if Tom left as soon as the speeches were over? She wouldn't have a chance to say goodbye to him properly, Imogen realised in a sudden panic. She didn't want to say it in front of everyone after all. She wanted to tell him what he had meant to her, but how could she do that with them all watching? *I love you* wasn't the kind of thing you could say with an audience.

Someone was chinking a glass, and the room fell silent while Imogen was still feverishly trying to work out how she could tell Tom what she felt. All at once it was imperative that she did. How could she have even thought she could go away without saying anything?

She barely heard the Director of HR introducing Tom, but she saw Tom take a step forward and clear his throat. He looked very grim, as if he would rather be almost anywhere else, and Imogen didn't blame him.

Tom looked at the sea of faces turned expectantly towards him. They were all waiting for him to deliver the usual tribute: always ready with a smile…will be much missed…wishing her all the best on her travels, blah, blah, blah. Tom had it all ready but, as he opened his mouth, he realised that he couldn't do it. He couldn't trot out some bland speech to Imogen. He couldn't pretend that she was just like everyone else when his heart was seething with the truth.

'You're all here because, even though Imogen hasn't been here very long, she's become part of the company,' he began slowly. 'She's been a good colleague to you and I'm sure you're going to miss her, but you're not going to miss her the way I will. When Imogen walks out of the door tonight, it's going to be like a light in my life that's been switched off.'

There was a sudden riveted silence in the room as everyone did a double take and checked with their neighbour that they hadn't misheard.

'The thing is, I've got used to her smile, to the way she sucks in her breath when she's annoyed.' Tom could hardly believe what he was saying, but the words just kept coming. 'I'll miss how she laughs on the phone, the perfume that she always wears. I'll miss the way my heart stops whenever she walks into the room, and how the day seems brighter and better when she's there.'

The room had fallen utterly silent by now, but Tom had forgotten everyone else. His attention was fixed on Imogen, who had been pushed to the front and was staring at him, blue eyes enormous. Now that he had started, it was easy, he realised. All he had to do was tell her everything that had been churning inside him since they'd returned from Coconut Island.

'I'm sorry if I'm embarrassing you,' he told her. 'If it's any comfort, I know I'm making the most colossal fool of myself too, but I just can't let you go without telling you how I feel. I've tried not to need you. I told myself that I would soon get used to it once you'd gone, but it's too late for me now. If you're not there, I can't get comfortable, nothing seems quite right, and when I look at what my life will be without you, I don't see success, I just see a flat, empty tundra I have to get across somehow.'

Imogen was still staring incredulously. Tom didn't blame her. He had never taken such a risk before, had never felt as if he were at the mercy of forces beyond his control the way he did now. He was terrified.

'I love you,' he told her, without taking his eyes from hers. 'There, I've said it! I didn't want to fall in love with you—I didn't think I *could*—and I've been trying to persuade myself that what we had on Coconut Island was just a temporary thing. I told myself this feeling would go away, but, Imogen, I don't think it's going to,' said Tom quietly. 'I think I'm going to spend the rest of my life missing you and the way you make me feel.

'I wasn't going to say anything,' he went on after a moment. 'I thought it would be awkward and embarrassing for both of us—as indeed it has been!' he added with a rueful smile. 'But you told me once that sometimes we have to be prepared to fail, and I guess that's what I'm doing now, but I don't want you to go without telling you what you've done for me. You've changed my life. I didn't understand when you told me that you were looking for someone who would complete you, but I do now. You've made me realise that I don't have your warmth and your laughter and that without them, without *you*, I'll never be quite right.'

He hesitated, wondering if he was making sense. 'I thought I was comfortable before. I thought I knew exactly what I wanted and what I needed to do, but the truth is that knowing you is the only thing that makes my life feel worthwhile.'

To his horror, Tom saw tears shining in Imogen's eyes. 'You don't need to worry,' he hurried on. 'I'm not expecting you to say anything. I know you've got plans, and I hope you'll have a wonderful time. You deserve to be happy. I just wanted…just wanted to thank you,' he said, losing the thread at last. 'For everything you've been, and everything you've done. I'll never forget you.'

There was another deafening silence. Nobody moved. They were clearly all waiting to see if he was planning on humiliating himself some more.

Imogen opened her mouth and then closed it again, unable to speak.

'Anyway,' said Tom too heartily, 'I believe we have a present for you.' He picked it up from the table and stood holding it, not sure what to do with it next.

He felt as if he had jumped off the edge of a cliff and was still bracing himself for a crash landing. It was a little late to realise that he had absolutely no idea of how he was going to get himself out of here.

But Imogen was moving at last. She stepped onto the dais while the entire room held its breath.

'I don't want a present,' she said very clearly, finding her voice at last. 'You've just given me everything I could ever want or ever need.'

Half the women in the room sighed.

Was that a smile tugging at the corners of her mouth? Hope began to beat wildly against Tom's ribs as he looked into Imogen's blue, blue eyes.

The Director of HR cleared his throat. 'I think perhaps Mr Maddison would like to say goodbye to Imogen alone,' he said firmly. 'The rest of us can continue the party in the pub.'

Reluctantly, people began to leave, looking over their shoulders at the scene at the front of the room, where Tom and Imogen stood facing each other, apparently oblivious to the room emptying.

Even when the door had closed behind the last of them and cut off the buzz of speculation outside, neither of them moved immediately.

'Sorry,' said Tom. 'Was that very embarrassing?'

'Very,' said Imogen unsteadily. 'And very beautiful.'

Stepping closer, she took the present from his nerveless hands and put it carefully on the table.

'Did you mean to say all that tonight?' she asked him.

He shook his head. 'I had another speech entirely prepared but, when it came to it, I realised I just couldn't do it. I couldn't say goodbye to you like that. I can't say goodbye to you at all.'

'Then don't.' Imogen closed the distance between them at last. Putting her arms round his neck, she pressed her face into his throat. 'Don't say goodbye, Tom. I can't bear it if you do.'

Instinctively, Tom's arms closed around her and he drew her hard against him, breathing in the scent of her, savouring the warmth and softness of her, his head reeling with the relief of holding her again.

'Imogen…does that mean you'll stay?'

'I will if you want me.'

'Want you?' Tom laughed raggedly. 'Imogen, you have no idea how much I do! I'm so in love with you, I don't know what to do with myself. You've turned my life upside down, and now you're the only one who can put it all right again.'

'But I'm so ordinary,' Imogen protested, pulling back slightly to look up into his face.

'You're not ordinary,' he said. 'You're beautiful and warm and loving and true. Are you thinking about Julia?'

'Of course. You've got to admit we're very different, and she was so much more suitable for you.'

'Suitable, maybe,' said Tom, 'but she wasn't you, and she didn't make me feel alive the way you do. She didn't make me the kind of man who takes crazy risks like the one tonight, and when I was with her I didn't feel as if I was in the only place I wanted to be, the way I feel when I'm with you.'

He pulled her back against him, sliding his hands under her hair to hold her head still. 'If it comes to that, do you think I don't know that *I'm* not suitable for *you*? I just wish I could be the man you really want.'

'But you are.' Imogen put her fingers over his mouth. 'Tom, you are,' she told him.

'You said you weren't prepared to settle for anyone less than perfect,' he reminded her. 'I'm not perfect.'

'No, you're not. You're really quite difficult at times,' she said, softening her words with a smile, 'but I love you anyway. And I'm not perfect either, but when we were together…the way you make me feel…*that's* perfect.'

A smile started in the silver-grey eyes and spread slowly over his face. 'Do I make you feel like a dolphin?' he asked, half joking, half hopeful.

Imogen remembered the dolphins soaring out of the sparkling sea into the sunlight and smiled back at him. 'That's *exactly* how I feel when I'm with you!'

Tom kissed her then, a long, deep, hungry kiss that left her breathless and blissful, and when he broke for air she wound her arms around him and kissed him back, while joy spilt through her in a glorious, giddy rush.

Imogen never knew how long they kissed there, or at what point they moved, but when she came up for air, Tom was leaning back against the desk and she was wedged between his legs. Heaving a sigh of happiness, she rested her head on his shoulder and felt his hands smoothing possessively up and down her spine.

'Why were you going to leave if you loved me?' he asked.

'Because I was afraid that if I stayed I would end up compromising. You'd been so certain that you would never fall in love, and I could see myself spending years just hoping and hoping that the impossible would happen.'

'The way you did with Andrew?'

She nodded against his shoulder. 'I told myself I had to face reality, and I didn't think I could do that, seeing you every day. I thought it would be easier to go to Australia, where there were no memories, and then you stood up there in front of all those people and told me that you loved me and I thought my heart was going to burst. I still can't believe this isn't a dream,' she confessed.

'If it is, we're both in it,' said Tom, kissing her softly. 'Now we've both got to face the reality of loving each other.'

Imogen nestled closer. 'That's one reality I don't mind facing!'

'Then we'll face it together.' He rested his check against her hair. 'Do you remember that ceremony on the sandbar?'

As if she could forget! 'That's when I first knew I loved you,' Imogen said, loving the feeling of being held tight against his hard, solid body. Of feeling safe. Of feeling cherished. 'I meant every word I said that day and I'm like you, I keep my promises.'

'I'm glad to hear it,' said Tom. 'So shall we make it legal and get married properly?'

Imogen's eyes were shining as she tipped back her head and smiled up at him. 'Yes, let's do that,' she said, and the warmth in his expression as he smiled back made her heart turn over.

'And where would you like to go on honeymoon?' he asked.

Imogen laughed, remembering how he had asked her that once before on a wet January day. 'We've already had a honeymoon!'

'We'll have another,' said the workaholic. 'I'll arrange it all. It just so happens that I know the perfect place…'

The old man was waiting for them on the sandbar, just like before. The sky was flushed with a gold that was just beginning to burn red. Tom took Imogen's hand and they walked across the sand towards him.

They had been married the week before in the little church in the village where Imogen had grown up. That had been a traditional wedding, and a very happy day, surrounded by family and friends, but the ceremony on the sandbar was just for the two of them.

It was six months since they had last been on Coconut Island, but the lagoon was as beautiful as ever. They spent their days just as they had done before, and in the evenings they sat on the veranda and watched the bats come out after sunset. It was all just the same—except this time Tom was her husband, not her boss, and Imogen hadn't known it was possible to be this happy.

Imogen had loved her wedding, but deep down it felt as if it wasn't until they had been through this ceremony again that she and Tom would really be married. She was wearing the wedding dress that had looked elegant and summery in the village church, but which she had chosen with the sandbar in mind. This time she was barefoot, and the chiffon layers stirred around her in the light ocean breeze as she laced her fingers with Tom's and stepped into the circle with him.

This time there was no hesitation, no awkwardness.

This time it was real.

If the old man thought it was odd that they were apparently renewing their vows so soon, he gave no sign of it. He went through the ceremony with quiet dignity and this time every word resonated along Imogen's veins.

'Love each other, be true to each other, find peace in each other,' he finished at last. 'Find joy in each other always.'

Tom and Imogen smiled as they drew together for a kiss. 'We will,' they said.

* * * * *

Celebrate 60 years of pure reading pleasure
with Harlequin®!

Harlequin Presents® is proud to introduce its
gripping new miniseries,
THE ROYAL HOUSE OF KAREDES.
An exquisite coronation diamond, split as a symbol of a
warring royal family's feud, is missing! But whoever
reunites the diamond halves will rule all....

Welcome to eight brand-new titles that unfold to reveal the
stories of kings and queens, princes and princesses torn
apart by pride and power, but finally reunited by love.

Step into the world of Karedes with
BILLIONAIRE PRINCE, PREGNANT MISTRESS
Available July 2009 from Harlequin Presents®.

ALEXANDROS KAREDES, SNOW DUSTING the shoulders of his leather jacket and glittering like jewels in his dark hair, stood at the door. Maria felt the blood drain from her head.

"Good evening, Ms. Santos."

His voice was as she remembered it. Deep. Husky. Perfect English, but with the faintest hint of a Greek accent. And cold, as cold as it had been that awful morning she would never forget, when he'd accused her of horrible things, called her terrible names....

"Aren't you going to ask me in?"

She fought for composure. Last time they'd faced each other, they'd been on his turf. Now they were on hers. She was in command here, and that meant everything.

"There's a sign on the door downstairs," she said, her tone every bit as frigid as his. "It says, 'No soliciting or vagrants.'"

His lips drew back in a wolfish grin. "Very amusing."

"What do you want, Prince Alexandros?"

A tight smile eased across his mouth and it killed her that even now, knowing he was a vicious, arrogant man, she couldn't help but notice what a handsome mouth it was. Chiseled. Generous. Beautiful, like the rest of him, which made him living proof that beauty could, indeed, be only skin deep.

"Such formality, Maria. You were hardly so proper the last time we were together."

She knew his choice of words was deliberate. She felt her face heat; she couldn't help that but she damned well didn't have to let him lure her into a verbal sparring match.

"I'll ask you once more, your highness. What do you want?"

"Ask me in and I'll tell you."

"I have no intention of asking you in. Tell me why you're here or don't. It's your choice, just as it will be my choice to shut the door in your face."

He laughed. It infuriated her but she could hardly blame him. He was tall—six two, six three—and though he stood with one shoulder leaning against the door frame, hands tucked casually into the pockets of the jacket, his pose was deceptive. He was strong, with the leanly muscled body of a well-trained athlete.

She remembered his body with painful clarity. The feel of him under her hands. The power of him moving over her. The taste of him on her tongue.

Suddenly, he straightened, his laughter gone. "I have not come this distance to stand in your doorway," he said coldly, "and I am not going to leave until I am ready to do so. I suggest you stand aside and stop behaving like a petulant child."

A petulant child? Was that what he thought? This man who had spent hours making love to her and had then accused her of—of trading her body for profit?

Except it had not been love, it had been sex. And the sooner she got rid of him, the better.

She let go of the doorknob and stepped aside. "You have five minutes."

He strolled past her, bringing cold air and the scent of the night with him. She swung toward him, arms folded. He reached past her, pushed the door closed, then folded his arms, too. She wanted to open the door again but she'd be damned if she was going to get into a who's-in-charge-here argument with him. She was in charge, and he would surely see a tussle over the ground rules as a sign of weakness.

Instead, she looked past him at the big clock above her work table.

"Ten seconds gone," she said briskly. "You're wasting time, your highness."

"What I have to say will take longer than five minutes."

"Then you'll just have to learn to economize. More than five minutes, I'll call the police."

Instantly, his hand was wrapped around her wrist. He tugged her toward him, his dark-chocolate eyes almost black with anger.

"You do that and I'll tell every tabloid shark I can contact about how Maria Santos tried to buy a five-hundred-thousand-dollar commission by seducing a prince." He smiled thinly. "They'll lap it up."

* * * * *

What will it take for this billionaire prince to realize he's falling in love with his mistress…?
Look for
BILLIONAIRE PRINCE, PREGNANT MISTRESS
by Sandra Marton
Available July 2009 from Harlequin Presents®.

We'll be spotlighting a different series every month throughout 2009 to celebrate our 60th anniversary.

Look for Harlequin® Presents in July!

TWO CROWNS, TWO ISLANDS, ONE LEGACY
A royal family, torn apart by pride and its lust for power, reunited by purity and passion

Step into the world of Karedes beginning this July with

BILLIONAIRE PRINCE, PREGNANT MISTRESS
by
Sandra Marton

Eight volumes to collect and treasure!

HARLEQUIN
Super Romance®

THE BELLES OF TEXAS

They're as strong as the state that raised
them. The Belle sisters aren't afraid to go
after what they want, whether it's reclaiming
their ranch or their family.

Linda Warren
CAITLYN'S PRIZE

Thanks to her deceased father's gambling
debts, Caitlyn Belle's beloved High Five Ranch
is in dire straits. Particularly because the
will stipulates that if the ranch doesn't turn
a profit in six months, it must be sold to
Judd Calhoun—the man Caitlyn jilted
fourteen years ago. And Cait knows Judd has
been waiting a long time for his revenge….

*Look for the first book
in The Belles of Texas miniseries,
on sale in July wherever books are sold.*

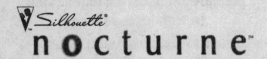

REQUEST YOUR FREE BOOKS!
2 FREE NOVELS PLUS 2
FREE GIFTS!

HARLEQUIN® *Romance*®

From the Heart, For the Heart

YES! Please send me 2 FREE Harlequin® Romance novels and my 2 FREE gifts (gifts are worth about $10). After receiving them, if I don't wish to receive any more books, I can return the shipping statement marked "cancel". If I don't cancel, I will receive 4 brand-new novels every month and be billed just $3.84 per book in the U.S. or $4.24 per book in Canada. That's a savings of at least 15% off the cover price! It's quite a bargain! Shipping and handling is just 50¢ per book.* I understand that accepting the 2 free books and gifts places me under no obligation to buy anything. I can always return a shipment and cancel at any time. Even if I never buy another book, the two free books and gifts are mine to keep forever.

114 HDN EYU3 314 HDN EYKG

Name	(PLEASE PRINT)	
Address		Apt. #
City	State/Prov.	Zip/Postal Code

Signature (if under 18, a parent or guardian must sign)

Mail to the **Harlequin Reader Service:**
IN U.S.A.: P.O. Box 1867, Buffalo, NY 14240-1867
IN CANADA: P.O. Box 609, Fort Erie, Ontario L2A 5X3

Not valid to current subscribers of Harlequin Romance books.

**Are you a subscriber of Harlequin Romance books
and want to receive the larger-print edition?
Call 1-800-873-8635 today!**

* Terms and prices subject to change without notice. Prices do not include applicable taxes. Sales tax applicable in N.Y. Canadian residents will be charged applicable provincial taxes and GST. Offer not valid in Quebec. This offer is limited to one order per household. All orders subject to approval. Credit or debit balances in a customer's account(s) may be offset by any other outstanding balance owed by or to the customer. Please allow 4 to 6 weeks for delivery. Offer available while quantities last.

Your Privacy: Harlequin Books is committed to protecting your privacy. Our Privacy Policy is available online at www.eHarlequin.com or upon request from the Reader Service. From time to time we make our lists of customers available to reputable third parties who may have a product or service of interest to you. If you would prefer we not share your name and address, please check here. ☐

HR09R